CAN'T DESIGN ME LOVE

A Natural State Romance

LEAH BREWER

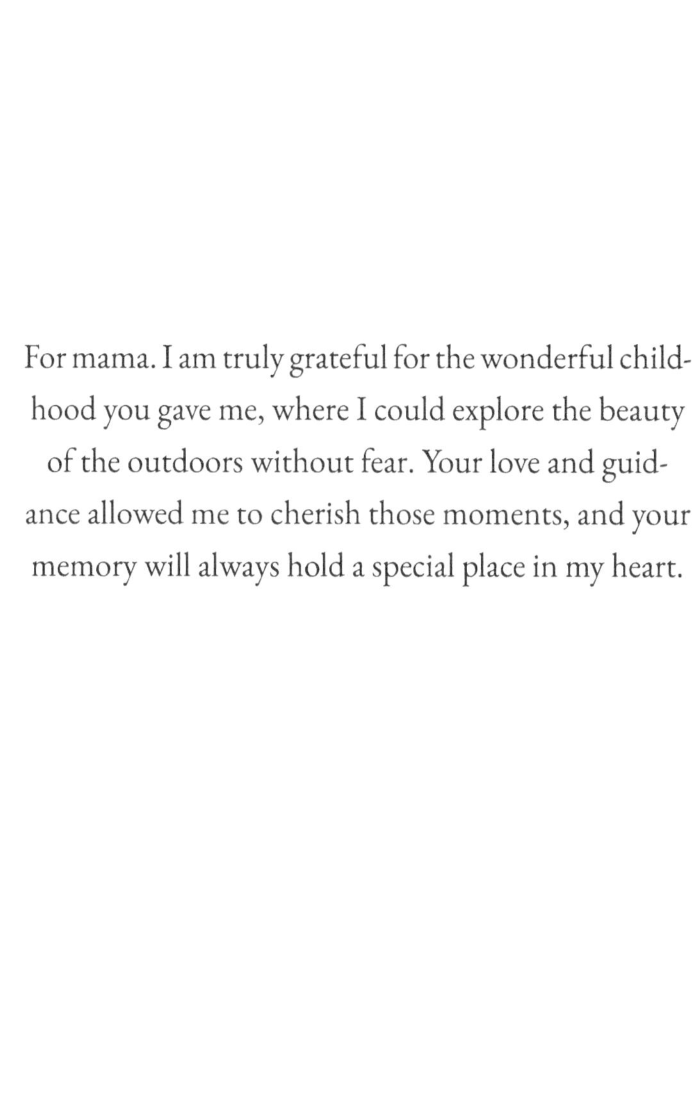

For mama. I am truly grateful for the wonderful childhood you gave me, where I could explore the beauty of the outdoors without fear. Your love and guidance allowed me to cherish those moments, and your memory will always hold a special place in my heart.

Also by Leah Brewer

Note From Leah

Growing up in DeValls Bluff was such a big part of my life. I'll never forget when my mom and I lived on a houseboat! It was one of the happiest times of my childhood.

Even though the Castleberry Hotel hasn't been operational for ages, I dream of seeing it restored! It's recognized as a national landmark, yet it needs so much love. That's what inspired me to include it in this book. I poured my hopes and dreams into these pages, and if there are any designers out there who want to help bring those dreams to life, I'd love to hear from you! The setting would make for a great reality show!

Every word I penned brought back many beautiful memories. Thank you for reading!

Chapter 1

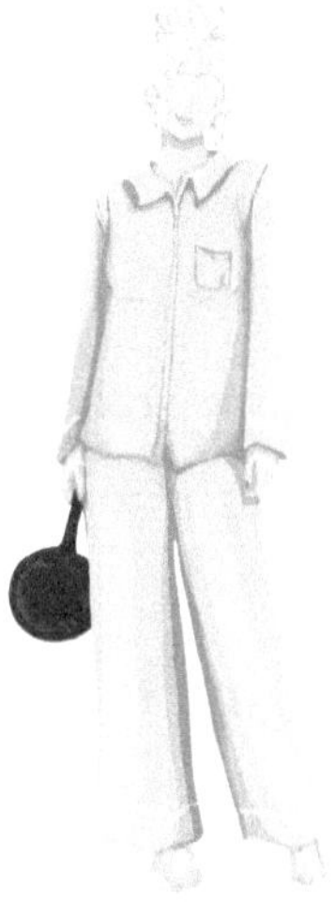

The haunting echo of glass shattering downstairs jolts me out of a deep sleep. A man yelps.

I grab my phone and quickly dial 911.

"911, what is your emergency?"

"Someone just broke in. My cousin and I are at the Banks cabin by the river, and there's a man downstairs!" Glancing out the bedside window, the moon hangs in a dark sky. This is the perfect time for a thief to be out doing what they do best.

After giving the address, the 911 operator's calm voice cuts through my thoughts, "Ma'am? The police are on their way."

My mind races. Did I forget to set the alarm? Could the bumbling burglar be smart enough to have disabled it? Will the police get here in time?

Shawna, my cousin's sleepy voice fills the air. "Jane, what's wrong?"

"There's someone downstairs, but the police will be here soon. In the meantime, I'm going to find a weapon."

"Please don't engage. Just hide," the operator says.

"I'm sorry, but we're sitting ducks if we stay in this room," I say, handing my phone to Shawna. "Hold this while I find a weapon."

A thud is followed by a series of grunts.

It sounds like whoever is downstairs crashed into the table I moved to the foyer yesterday. He must've knocked the lamp over.

My heart kicks up a notch. My Aunt Olivia would kill me if I let anything happen to Shawna. Besides, I've never known a more incompetent burglar. Even though I don't know many burglars, this one is the worst. It's like he's not even trying to conceal his presence. So, I can easily get the jump on him. He must think the place is empty since the owners, Clara and Archer Banks, live in Las Vegas. We're only staying here because I'm in a design competition that's being filmed here in DeValls Bluff, Arkansas.

Grabbing my pink silk pajamas, I put them on over my vintage My Little Pony nightgown.

"Who do you think it is, Jane?" she whispers.

"Hush, I need to listen," I whisper back before putting a finger to my mouth, as I creep down the dark stairs, Shawna right behind me.

My mind races with a whirlwind of possibilities, each more unsettling than the last. Here I am, in a secluded cabin on the banks of the White River. It's past midnight, and the only company I have is my younger cousin, Shawna. With a clenched jaw, I stop just outside the door to the kitchen, shadows flickering in the dim light of the moon.

My gaze locks onto the iron skillet I left on the counter after cooking fried potatoes earlier. I wrap my fingers around the handle, its cool metal grounding me for a moment. Signaling for Shawna to follow, I lead her into the pantry, the small space filled with cereal and other boxed goods we bought. How close this pantry is to the staircase is a stroke of luck.

My heart pounds as I lean in, straining to listen for any hint of movement in the living room. The sofa screeches as it skids across the floor before the intruder moans. I'm glad I rearranged the living room. At least it slowed him down.

Leaning close to Shawna's ear, I lower my voice as much as possible. "Stay here. I need to see who this is."

"Okay," she says, a slight tremor in her voice.

As I tiptoe out of the pantry, my forehead furrows. How dare someone come into my best friend's cabin and try to rob it and scare my cousin?

He comes closer to the kitchen.

I take a deep breath.

My weapon is ready.

I'm ready.

The burglar has no idea what's coming. He broke into the wrong cabin. Not only is he about to face a skillet, but the person holding it has played almost as many baseball games as Nolan Ryan.

A trickle of fear runs down my spine, followed by a surge of determination. What if someone saw Shawna and me and decided to break in here to kidnap us?

No one here is going to take either of us, that's for sure.

My grip tightens on the handle, and I raise the skillet like I'm up next to bat. I spread my legs and get ready to knock the robber out.

A dark shadow crosses over the wall behind me. I press my back against the wall behind the massive dining cabinet. It's the perfect spot to ambush the robber.

Come a little closer. Just a few more steps, buddy, and you're meeting your Maker.

The footsteps stop.

I lunge from my hiding spot and swing the bat, er, the skillet. It cracks them in the hand. The robber lets out a yip. Raising the skillet for the knockout, I aim for their head this time.

Midair, the skillet gets snatched from my hand, and the burglar pushes me against the wall. Hard. I catch a whiff of rich citrus. Why does he smell so good?

Shawna screams as she bolts out of the pantry. "Get off my cousin!" she says right before she jumps on the robber's back.

I flip the light on, prepared to fight for our lives. The scene before me is not what I expected.

Shawna is pounding on the chest of none other than Donny Sharp, my best friend's annoying younger brother.

His green eyes light up with a sparkle as his gaze settles on my nightgown beneath the silk pajama top, now hanging wide open. "Now, Jane, if you wanted to get up close and personal with me, all you had to do was ask."

Shawna stands up, her face as red as the blood flowing from Donny's hand.

Wait. Blood?

"What happened?" I ask, like I've lost my marbles.

He winces. "I think you broke my hand with that stupid skillet, there, Chuck Norris."

Blue lights surround us before footsteps stomp onto the wrap-around porch. "Police! Open up!"

With a heavy sigh, I lean my head back and stare at the ceiling. I bet I never live this one down.

Chapter 2

As the lead singer of Donny Sharp and the Nostalgic Echoes, a local Arkansas band, I've met quite a few flirtatious women, but nothing compares to the girl pursuing me now. After her little stunt last week, I decided to visit my college friend, Jesse Austin, a local police officer.

When my sister married a hotshot football player with a vacation rental company, she became the owner of an incredible cabin on the White River in the tiny town of DeValls Bluff, Arkansas. After calling my brother-in-law, Archer, he said I could stay here.

Never in a million years did I imagine that the night I came, Jane Gorgeous Bennett would be here. Okay, her middle name isn't really Gorgeous, but that's how I've thought of her since I was fourteen.

My hand throbs, and I want to cry, but I will eat the skillet Jane has in her hand before that happens. Flashing blue lights shine through the windows. "Police! Open up!"

Jane's My Little Pony nightgown hangs out over her silky pajama set. One thing I adore about Jane is she's a total eighties girl. She's dressed as if she walked right out of an eighties-based movie set since she was a teenager.

I shoot a glance at Jane from the corner of my eye. "Someone better let the police in before they break the door down."

Jane's cousin Shawna, I think, scrambles toward the door, her face still flushed. "I will let the police in. Okay, Jane?"

Jane shakes her head. "Shawna, let Donny open the door." She says as she slips the skillet behind her back. With a narrowed gaze, she nods at the door that was getting pounded on. "Door, please."

"Yes, ma'am," I say with a grin.

I move past Shawna before swinging the door open, my hands in the air as blood drips down my wrist. In the last episode of Cops I watched, the man who opened the door had his hands up, so that's what I do, even though my hand is practically numb. I can't help but smile bigger when I lock eyes with Jesse Austin, my old college buddy.

He lowers his weapon and cocks his head. "Donny? When you said you were coming for a visit, I had no idea you'd start trouble on your first night here." He grins before glancing at my bloody hand. His spine tenses, and he says, "What happened?"

I move back a step, flashing a reassuring smile. "Oh, it's just a minor misunderstanding. Come on in."

Jesse walks in right behind me, still holding his gun, but at least it's pointed down now.

I grab a hand towel with frayed edges from the kitchen counter and turn to him as I wrap my bleeding hand.

He puts his gun away with a quick motion. "So, what went down here?" he asks, his voice calm, but I can tell he's worried. He nods toward Jane. "I know you're here for the competition," he says, then turns to me. "And I know you were planning on making a visit soon. How did you both end up at this cabin with you bleeding?"

Jane and I exchange a glance, and I figure we look guilty of some wrongdoing.

Before either of us speaks, Jesse tilts his head, his eyes zeroing in on Jane. "Is that a skillet?"

"Uh, totally! It's definitely a skillet," Jane replies, a trace of nervousness creeping into her tone as she rubs the back of her neck. "You know I whipped up some fried potatoes for supper earlier!"

Shawna's chin trembles with urgency. "Please don't take Jane to jail! I swear she didn't mean to hurt Donny!"

Jane moves close to Shawna and puts a reassuring hand on her arm. "Technically, I meant to hurt Donny, but I thought he was a burglar. See, I'm here for the competition, and this is my best friend's cabin. I'm assuming Donny didn't know I was here, or he wouldn't be here."

Despite the palpable tension hanging in the air, a warmth spreads through my chest as Jane flounders in her attempt to explain away the mishap. Her cheeks flush a soft pink, and she blows a stray golden curl away from her forehead, only for it to cling to her face, a few strands slipping free from her messy bun. The clumsiness of her words only adds to her charm, and not knowing how adorable she looks, she rambles on, her voice a mix of nervousness and determination. She always did this growing up, and I see it's a habit she's never quite shaken.

I can't help but smile at the sight of her, with tousled hair spilling from her messy bun into her eyes. No one else could look so effortlessly attractive while wearing a forty-year-old My Little Pony nightgown and wielding a heavy skillet. All this, on top of the fact that Jane is the one person I've always wanted to date but never could, makes the moment almost surreal.

When the EMT arrives, I feel a wave of relief. She's super friendly as she examines my cut. "You're in luck. If you need stitches, it'll only be a few," she says with an upbeat tone.

"Stitches?" Nah, I don't think so. "Jesse, do you have any glue?"

"I have some Dermabond in my cruiser."

"That'll work." When the EMT puts her chunky hand on her hip, I grin. "I promise I'll get it checked out in the morning."

"It's not like I can force you to see a doctor, but I highly recommend it," she says.

I flash another smile. "Thank you for your help."

An hour later, my cut glued shut, Jesse and I laugh about the situation while I walk him to his police car. I can't help but smile as I look at the white bandage on my hand. We stop at his cruiser, parked right beside my trusty black Ford F-150.

When I slip back inside, Shawna has her head in Jane's lap, and they're both fast asleep. I take a sip of water as I settle into the recliner.

Will Jane want me here? Maybe she'll let me stay in the bedroom upstairs since Shawna is here to chaperone. As I'm thinking of how to talk her into letting me stay, she opens her eyes. The same deep brown eyes I've wanted to lose myself in for as long as I can remember. I gulp and shift my weight, pulling a leg beneath me.

She lifts her chin and stares at me for a few seconds. "Shawna and I are sharing one of the guest rooms, so you can take the main bedroom."

"So, I can stay?" I ask, raising my brow as I lean the recliner back.

She lowers her gaze and sighs. "Yes, you can stay. For tonight at least."

"I kind of have plans with Jesse this weekend, and there aren't many hotels in DeValls Bluff, you know."

She narrows her eyes but doesn't answer.

"Look, I'll do my best not to bother you. This cabin is big enough for us all to be here, and you'd be doing me a huge favor if you let me stay." I continue my rambling.

"I do feel terrible for what happened." She sighs again, as if my request is unreasonable.

"Pretty please," I beg while attempting to give her a smoldering look that usually causes women to giggle and act silly.

"You had better stay out of my way," she says, ignoring my smolder like she always has. "I guess someone needs to make sure you're fed since you're hurt."

With sheer willpower, I stop myself from jumping up and doing a happy dance. Instead, I wink at Jane. "You saying you're gonna be cooking for me?"

Her cheeks turn pink, and she bolts off the light brown leather sofa. Shawna's head rolls to the side. Jane gasps, leaning over Shawna. Suddenly, she swivels around, wagging her finger at me. "I will help you all I can since this is my fault, but my focus is winning the competition, so you'd better be on your best behavior."

I stand, saluting Jane with my uninjured hand. "Yes, ma'am."

Jane sticks her feet into fluffy pink slippers and leans close to Shawna. "Shawna, let's go to bed," she says, her tone so soft it makes my heart melt in my chest.

Shawna rubs her eyes as Jane guides her out of the room. "Okay, I'm sleepy."

"I know," Jane says, their voices fading as they disappear down the hallway.

After having a crush on Jane since middle school, maybe I have a real chance of getting her to go on a date with me. I never would've guessed I'd be so happy to be mistaken for a burglar.

Chapter 3

As I slice through the plump, crimson strawberries, my mind wanders from sketching vivid houseboat designs good enough to move on to the finale to replaying the events of the previous night. The fresh aroma of the strawberries fills the air, mingling with the cheesy, sizzling eggs in the same skillet I used to smack Donny.

On my iPhone screen, a charismatic chef details his secrets to achieving the perfect omelet, gesturing as he emphasizes the importance of using just the right amount of butter and whisking the eggs until they're frothy.

I swear I've watched the video six times. Why am I doing this? I should be working on my design, not thinking about my best friend's brother. Especially not making him breakfast. Most definitely not thinking about how much he reminded me of the lead singer in my favorite eighties rock band last night. My heart speeds up. I take a few slow, deep breaths and repeat that I can never date Donny Sharp. The thought of dating a younger man gives love a bad name, that's for sure. I've always been against dating someone younger than me. I'm more into older men. Men who know what they want and how to get it. I don't need little boys who act like teenagers. No, thank you.

I jump a little when a FaceTime call comes in from the very best friend, who's been on my mind. With a nervous laugh, I answer the call and prop up the phone against the cheese package. "What's up?"

Clara cocks her head, allowing her dark curls to cascade down her shoulders. "Are you okay?"

Heat covers my neck, and I cringe. Why am I being

so weird? I'd better get my stuff together before Clara suspects something. Not that there's anything to suspect. Nothing. "Yeah, I was trying to make an omelet, but it's turned into scrambled eggs."

Her eyes widen, and she leans forward like she's trying to see further into the kitchen. "Why?"

"Why, what?" I ask as I toss another egg into the skillet, then whisk it into the egg mixture with milk and cheese.

"Why are you making food? You never cook for anyone." Clara taps her chin, and a sly smile appears. "Who are you trying to impress?"

"No one," I reply a little too quickly, my voice coming out like a barn owl calling its mate. "And yes, I cook. All the time. Ask Shawna about the fried potatoes I made just last night."

"Um, no, you don't cook all the time." She raises her hands to make air quotes around the phrase. "Yeah, maybe you made fried potatoes, but when's the last time you made breakfast? Did you ever cook for Chance?"

"Chance and I didn't date very long, remember?" I leave the phone on the counter and walk to the refrigerator, grabbing a jug of orange juice. "Stop grilling me about breakfast and tell me why you called. Is my future goddaughter doing well?"

"Your future goddaughter *or* godson is doing great," she says with a smile. "But I really wanna talk about this breakfast thing..."

Donny chooses that moment to pop up behind me. He snatches a strawberry before grinning at Clara. "Hey, sis!"

Clara turns away from the screen. "Archer, Donny is at the cabin with Jane," she says before giving us her attention. "Donny. I've tried calling you."

He scoots back into the phone screen, which is a little too close for comfort. "Sorry, I turned my phone off before I left Little Rock last night."

I scoot over as Clara asks, "Why?"

"I have my reasons," Donny vaguely replies, which makes me wonder what those reasons could be.

"Well, turn it on and read my texts."

"I'll think about it."

"I see Jane let you spend the night," Clara says with a grin so large her cheeks are sure to burst.

"Yep."

"And she's making you eggs for breakfast."

The heat covering my neck now feels like I imagine

the coal in a wood-burning fireplace would feel. "I was planning to make breakfast anyway," I say as I set the orange juice on the counter before meeting Clara's gaze.

I'm sure she's on the verge of calling me a liar. Instead, she surprises me with, "I have an appointment, so I'd better run. I just wanted to see how last night went."

My hand flies to my hip. "Wait. Did you know Donny was coming here?"

"Gotta go. By-eeeee," she says before the call ends.

I turn to Donny. "Did your sister know you were coming?"

He shrugs before popping another strawberry into his mouth.

After moving the eggs to a plate, I meet his gaze. "She did, didn't she?"

"Did you really make me breakfast? Thank you," he says, ignoring my question, with a wince.

I drop my gaze to his hand, which is still bandaged. "Are you in pain? Can I help you with anything?"

"It'll be fine," he says as he leans toward the stove. "I'm starving, and those eggs look good."

"Take a seat, and I'll make you a plate."

"Really?"

"Yes, sit."

A few minutes later, Shawna, Donny, and I have plates full of eggs and strawberries. It may not be the omelet I intended, but it isn't half bad.

Shawna takes a drink of her chocolate milk and sets her fork down. "I'm happy that I'm here with you, Jane."

"I'm glad you're here, too."

"We are cousins and friends, even though you are so much older than I am, right?"

"Of course we are." The bite of eggs goes down my throat like a cat falling into a bucket of water. Donny and Shawna are the same age. I almost let myself forget he is too young for me. Not that I was thinking of dating him or anything. He's not only three years younger, but he's also my best friend's little brother. I've known Donny since he was in daycare.

What kind of person am I?

I harden my heart as much as possible because I'm a person who will absolutely not fall for her best friend's younger brother.

That's so cheesy romance novel type behavior, and I'm not here for it.

Chapter 4

After Jane and Shawna head out to work on Jane's design for the competition, I have a moment to myself.

I sit down and peel the bandage off my hand, wincing at the burning sensation. Pain isn't anything new to me.

There was that one time when I skidded down the side of a mountain on my bike and crashed into a jagged tree branch. Now that hurt. I still have an impressive scar running down my leg from that adventure.

Compared with that, this minor cut is manageable.

With the bandage off, I turn on my phone and wait as a flood of notifications begins.

Ignoring everyone else for now, I scroll through until I find my sister's name.

CLARA

Are you going to the DVB cabin?

Archer said you are.

When are you leaving?

Hellooooo

Answer me.

JANE IS THERE!

Even though we spoke a bit this morning, I figure I'd better answer her.

DONNY

Sorry, but my agent wouldn't leave me alone

> So, I turned my phone off.

> The girl I told you about a couple of months ago is obsessed with me

My phone immediately rings with a FaceTime. "Wow, that was fast," I grin into the phone.

A line creases Clara's brow as she frowns. "Who is obsessed with you?"

"Do you remember me telling you about the seventeen-year-old girl from Rogers who ambushed me at Top Golf?"

"Yeah. What did she do?"

I run my hand through my shoulder-length hair. "Well, she turned eighteen last month, and she's been coming to every show and buying backstage passes."

Clara leans back on her sofa. "I mean, that's not too bad, unless you're not telling me everything?"

"Well," I say, rubbing my finger across the red guitar pick necklace Dad made from a pick he'd gotten at a Journey concert. "She followed me to my apartment last weekend."

"Wait one stinking minute," Clara says as she bolts off the sofa, phone in hand. "Did you say she followed you home?"

"Yeah, I was just getting out of the shower when the doorbell rang. It was almost three in the morning by then." I move my head back and forth as the incident plays over in my mind like a scene from Fatal Attraction.

Clara gasps. "Please tell me you didn't open the door."

"Of course I didn't. I have a camera pointed at my door, so I saw who it was."

"What did you do?"

"I ignored her."

Her lips press into a flat line. "You should've called the police, Donny."

"My neighbor beat me to it."

"Oh, well, that's good."

"I mean, I had to open the door when they got there, and they assumed I'd done something to this girl." I clench my jaw, every muscle taut with the memory of having to defend myself.

"What?" Disbelief rang in her tone.

"Yeah, I had to give them my camera feed and explain how she's been trying to date me for a while."

"That makes me madder than a wet hen."

If I weren't so frustrated, I'd give Clara a hard time about her use of Arkansas slang. "Her parents called me and apologized, and I agreed not to press charges, but then yesterday she posted about me on social media."

"No way."

I stand, my heart racing as I pace back and forth from the window to the bed. "Yes way. She has a video of our first meeting that shows me smiling at her."

"You have got to be kidding me."

"People are commenting about how sorry I am to have led her on and how I should be ashamed of myself for treating her like that." I knock a half-empty glass of ice water off my side table. "Maybe I need to find a different career."

Clara narrows her eyes. "No, you need to make a statement."

"Why? It's not like I'm a famous musician or something. I'm in a band that travels around Arkansas playing cover songs from popular eighties rock bands."

"But look at your face."

My brow's pinch together as I cock my head. "My face?"

"Your smile drives women wild, and you know it.

When you find the woman of your dreams, smile at her, make her a pan of mom's lasagna, and you'll have her hooked in no time."

"Okay, weirdo. Listen, the doorbell just rang. Jesse and I are going fishing, so I need to get."

"Hey, Jane told me about your hand. Is the cut bad?"

"Nah, not too bad. We're gonna stop by the clinic in Hazen before we go fishing."

"Okay. You'd better clean whatever you knocked off your table up before you leave. Love you, little brother."

"Love you," I say, pitching the phone on the bed. With a glance at the water, I lay a towel over it and wipe it up.

A day of fishing on the White River sounds amazing. After that, I'll be making Jane a pan of lasagna for dinner.

Chapter 5

The tiny town of DeValls Bluff buzzes with activity as Shawna and I drive to the White River basin. Not only are the locals out, but people interested in seeing the design show have come out in full force.

When we arrive at the basin, I hop out of my pink Jeep and skip to the coffee truck. Technically, it's a bakery, but they serve excellent coffee. Cool air nips at my cheeks as I hustle toward my morning pick me up. Today I am extra thankful for the thick sweater I found at a vintage shop in Little Rock this past weekend. It goes perfectly with my red jeans and white high-top Converse.

I inhale the scent of cinnamon and freshly baked chocolate croissants. Even though it's a chilly start to the first week of March, I have a feeling today is going to be fantastic.

"I'm going to say hi to Maya," Shawna says as she heads toward the three other food trucks. She passes by Cindy's Home Cooking and Chinese Buffet on Wheels, before stopping at Maya's Burgers.

After a minute of speaking with her friend, Shawna meanders over and orders a sausage biscuit and hot cocoa, as I wait for my Lucky Charms latte.

My body tingles with energy as I peek at the houseboats sitting in the basin. Things are going great. Better than great. Not only am I in the top four of the design competition, but it's on the biggest TV station ever. I know the six I've beaten out so far were fantastic at what they do, so how is this my life?

I resist the urge to break into my favorite song as I skip down the walkway to the houseboat I'll be redoing for the competition. If I can pull it off, I'll be in the finale. As I step down into the main area, I stop fighting the urge and belt out, "Girls Just Wanna Have Fun" at the top of my lungs.

Shawna grins at me right before a scream slices through the air, followed by a splash. We race up the steps onto the deck just in time to see Nelly Harrington, my design assistant, sink into the murky water with a gurgle.

One of the new photographers, a man I've only met once, jumps in after her. Within a few minutes, Nelly and the photographer, whose name I can't remember, sit on the shore wrapped in blankets. The onsite nurse kneels beside a trembling Nelly and shakes her head.

"I can't feel my arm," Nelly says as tears pour down her face.

By the time an ambulance pulls into the parking area, I've guzzled my coffee and paced so much I've already met my steps goal.

Lisa Flowers, the director of Small Town, Big Design, waves her left hand as she screams into her phone, hangs up, and sprints to the ambulance.

Did I say today was going to be fantastic? I may have been off by a tiny bit.

By the time Shawna and I drag ourselves up the steps to the cabin, black clouds darken the sky. Shawna's stomach growls.

"Why don't we get cleaned up and go out for dinner?" I push open the front door.

The aroma of marinara sauce hits me as soon as I step inside. Donny's muscles strain against his long-sleeved t-shirt as he pulls a pan from the oven.

He sets it on the stove before turning toward us, a slow smile dancing across his face. "Hello, honey, I made dinner." He pins me with his gaze before turning to Shawna. "I hope the two of you are hungry."

Shawna marches over to Donny and pulls him into a quick hug. "You have no idea how hungry I am. My stomach just growled when we were outside."

"We just need a few minutes to freshen up," I say, careful to keep my tone light.

When we rejoin Donny, he ushers us to the table. I feel his gaze on me as I glance at the meal already set out. "This looks amazing. How did you do all this with your injured hand?"

"I used Mom's recipe," Donny says with a shrug. "And I was careful to keep my cut bandaged."

"I have autism," Shawna announces as we sit down.

Donny cocks his head. I hold my breath. He shrugs again. "I didn't know that," he says before laying his hand on top of hers. "It's also nothing you need to explain. You're my cool new friend, and that's all that matters."

Shawna smiles at Donny and then turns to me, beaming. I gulp a bite of lasagna down as my heart warms. For the first time, I look at Donny as a man, not just Clara's little brother. He's considerate, not to mention fine. Gorgeous, even.

My mind races with thoughts of his dreamy eyes. Dreamy? Seriously, Jane? Get a grip.

This is not good. Not even a little.

Chapter 6

"Thanks for making dinner," I say, glancing at Donny across the table. "It was almost as good as your mom's."

"Almost?" Donny asks, a smirk appearing on his face.

Shawna stands, pushing the Candy Land board away. "I think it was wonderful, but now I'm sleepy. I don't want to play anymore."

"That's fine, Shawna. I'll be in there in a little while."

Shawna taps her chin. "What are you going to do?"

"I need to make a list of people who can help with the houseboat, and then I can do the dishes."

She pauses for a moment, a thoughtful crease forming between her brows as she glances at the stack of dishes piled high in the sink. "I can do the dishes if you'd like," she offers.

Donny shakes his head, a reassuring smile spreading across his face. "That's really unnecessary," he replies, leaning against the table. "I'll load the dishwasher before I go to bed."

Shawna bites her lip. "Are you sure? I really don't mind helping," she insists.

"Positive," he assures her. "It's just a few dishes. Night, Shawna."

"Good night, bestie," she says, her tone warm as she turns to leave.

A smile dominates Donny's face as Shawna drifts through the door. "I really like her."

Ignoring the fact that my legs are melting to putty, I nod. "It would be hard not to like Shawna. I love how she doesn't let autism define her. She's very open about it because with or without it, she's proud of the person she is."

"I can see that." He rests his arm on the table, giving me his undivided attention. "You seem close."

"Oh yeah, we've grown a lot closer since my uncle Ray moved her and Aunt Olivia back to Arkansas last year," I say, twisting my hands together. "I love how blunt she is, but not only that, she's fierce. You know she'd do anything to protect the ones she loves."

"Yeah," he says, bobbing his head with a grin. "I experienced that firsthand when she tackled me in the kitchen."

I snort a laugh, picturing the scene vividly. "She really did think you were a burglar sneaking in here at midnight."

"Very true." Donny lifts himself out of the chair and carries Shawna's glass to the sink. "So, what's the story behind the houseboat?"

"First, let me set one thing straight," I begin, my tone firm as my gaze shifts to his injured hand, the bandage stark against his skin. "You are absolutely not loading the dishwasher."

He shakes his head, a stubborn glint in his eye as he slowly makes his way back to the table, determination etched on his features. "I can manage it just fine," he insists.

"Nope. You cooked a fantastic dinner, and let's be honest, your hand is probably aching right now after that little mishap with the skillet," I reply, gesturing toward his hand.

"It's fine," he shoots back, dismissing my concern with a shake of his head that's a bit too quick.

"Liar," I tease, my lips curling into a playful smile as I cross my arms.

"How about we do it together?" he suggests, his fingers absently tugging at the leather necklace around his neck.

Ignoring the fact that Donny's thick lashes frame his green eyes, I shrug as I wet a rag to wipe down the table. "Okay."

"So, what do you need help with on a houseboat?" he asks as he sprays the plates off.

"It's for the competition," I tell him about what happened with the design assistant and how I need to find someone to help quickly.

He dries his hands and picks up his sweet tea. "I'll do it."

I grunt and reach for my glass. "I couldn't ask you to do that."

"I insist. It'll give me something to do. I promise I'll

be a good boy." His expression softens, and he jiggles his brows. "Plus, this will give me a chance to win you over."

My heart skyrockets for some stupid reason. "Win me over? What are you talking about?"

"Doesn't that show you and Clara watch all the time say that a man in possession of a good fortune must be in want of a wife? Or something along those lines?"

My mouth hangs open as I lock my eyes onto him. "Huh?"

"I'm a man," he asserts, his hand sweeping confidently over his physique. A playful glint dances in his eyes as he adds, "And you look like the perfect candidate for a wife."

"You are not in possession of a fortune," I retort, a smirk playing at the corners of my lips as I fold my arms tightly over my chest. "And you're not a man. You're Clara's little brother."

The side of his mouth quirks upward. "But you think I'm hot, don't you?"

"You are such a flirt." I lean forward, busying my hands with boxing up the game before I finish wiping the table off.

Donny swaggers back over to the sink. He pivots

around, meeting my gaze. "What time should I be ready to leave in the morning?"

Clearly, he's unaware of how my mind is racing with those marriage comments. He's lost his mind. There's no way I could marry Donny Sharp. Not a chance. And I do not think he is hot.

Frowning, I narrow my gaze as I stop beside him at the sink. "Around eight, I guess."

"I'll be ready at seven." He smiles, making the small dark freckle at the corner of his top lip stand out.

Before I do something stupid, I grab the hand towel and swat his arm with it. "Scoot over, and I'll get the dishwasher loaded."

"Or what? You gonna hit me with a skillet again, Chuck?"

With a glance around the room, I snicker. "Don't tempt me. Luckily for you, I don't see the skillet."

He reaches out and grabs the hand towel, causing me to wobble on my feet. I snatch it away, and he steps closer, attempting to wrestle it out of my hand.

I giggle, and then *it* happens.

His hand brushes mine. My brain fizzles at the same time every skin cell misfires. I press my hand to my chest, trying to catch my breath.

I've had crushes and even thought I loved boys before, but in all my twenty-six years, I've never experienced a zing.

I've been waiting for this exact moment ever since watching Hotel Transylvania as a kid. I've dreamed of experiencing that euphoric zing moment, that perfect connection with someone like Mavis did with Johnny.

Why, oh, why did it have to happen with my best friend's younger brother? But the more pressing question is, what do I do about it?

Chapter 7

After a few weeks in DeValls Bluff, I can see why Jesse was so eager to move here from Little Rock. The people are friendly, and the area has a lot of appeal, especially for hunting and fishing. I bet with a little more targeted marketing, this town could be on postcards. But the best part for me is that Jane is letting me help her redo the houseboat.

My phone buzzes with an incoming call from Sebastian, my agent, as I pull into the basin. "What's up?"

"Donny, we have the opportunity to travel to Japan with Bloody Dragons!" The excitement in his voice comes through loud and clear.

The thing is, I would rather quit the band than travel that far. "Sebastian, I told you before you were ever hired that I will not under any circumstances travel internationally. Especially not to play with that weird band."

"The rest of the band feels differently."

"I don't care how they feel. The answer is no," I shoot back, a vein in my forehead throbbing.

"Look, you need to get over this little fear you have of flying."

"You need to mind your own business and do the job I hired you to do. Keep us local, or you can move on." I hit the end button and take a few breaths to stifle the embarrassment I always feel when my fear of flying gets brought up.

As I step out of my Ford, the wind blows a few strands of hair into my eyes, and I push them behind my ear. One of the crew members greets me as I climb onto the houseboat. With a wave, I take the few steps through the wide-open space toward the bathroom, where Jane and Shawna are.

Jane twists her body beneath the wall-mounted toilet and holds her hand out to Shawna. "Hand me the rag."

Shawna plops a rag in Jane's hand. "Did you fix it?"

"There wasn't a leak. Looks like the water came from the sink when we cleaned it earlier." Jane slides out from under the toilet to stand beside it. Her lips curl into a smile when she meets my gaze.

A burst of raindrops dances along the small window, and I have a sudden craving to curl up near the fireplace at the cabin with a heaping cup of cocoa and Jane. My gaze moves around the updated bathroom as I tamp my thoughts down. "The black and gray stone walls look good. They really stand out against the white shower," I say, sounding very much like an idiot.

"Thank you! I absolutely love the look, and if I remember correctly, you were the one who suggested the bold black stone," she says, running her fingers through her hair, her expression focused as she looks around the room.

With a bow and a grin, I say, "I am at your service, ready to help."

Jane's cheeks turn pink, and she swallows. "The bathroom is officially done."

Shawna scratches her head as she looks from me to Jane and back again. "I'm going to talk to Maya."

"Okay, see you soon." Jane follows closely behind. "Make sure you wear your rain jacket."

"Got it." Shawna snags a blue rain jacket and waves it in the air before she takes the steps two at a time.

Jane swivels and almost bumps into me. Maybe I'm standing a little too close for her comfort. Not for mine, though.

Our eyes lock onto each other. Her face still wears a slight smile, but I can tell underneath, she is struggling with her emotions. Could it be because of me? Maybe, just maybe, Jane has stronger feelings than she lets on.

Footsteps echo on the wooden stairs as a tall, blonde man enters the room with confidence. I can't help but think he looks like he just stepped off a romance novel cover. His hair catches the light, highlighting his chiseled features, and a flash of jealousy hits me when I see how long his gaze lingers on Jane.

A slight frown creases his brow before he reaches out to shake hands first with Jane, then with me. "You must be Jane Bennett," he says, his voice smooth and charming as I expected.

"That's me," Jane says, her voice brightening the room and pulling me out of my thoughts.

"Hi, I'm Theodore Baldwin, the new guest judge," he introduces himself, a warm smile spreading across his face that makes me think I imagined the frown from earlier.

"Who? I've never heard of you," she says, raising an eyebrow with genuine curiosity as she looks the newcomer over, a mix of interest and caution on her face.

"That's understandable," Theodore replies. "I am definitely no one you would've heard of."

I take a step closer to Jane, still uneasy about how he's watching her like a hawk. "How did you get this gig, then?"

"I own a furniture company that dabbles in home design in New York. Somehow, I've ended up hosting a reality design show that's set to premiere next month. They brought me on to help get people talking before it kicks off," he says with a shrug.

Somehow? Maybe the fact that he looks like a male model and sounds like he could have his pick of voiceover commercials played a part in him getting his new show.

I can't be jealous of a man who looks at least forty. Wait, how old is Jane again? She's the same age as my sister. Is forty too old for her? Technically, I guess they could date, but that would be terrible. Absolutely yes, he's too old, and that's my final answer.

"That's great. What's the name of your furniture company?" Jane takes a step closer to Theodore, causing my spine to work overtime on reaching the ceiling.

This won't cut it. Since the lasagna didn't work the way I thought it would, maybe I need to ask Gramma for some of her recipes.

Chapter 8

Theodore Baldwin, the new judge, looks so familiar that I'm sure I've ordered pieces from his furniture company, Baldwin Home.

"Have you heard of it?" Theodore slips his hands into the pockets of his pinstriped tan slacks.

"It's possible. I'll check your website out."

Donny steps so close to me that our shoulders touch. I stifle a giggle as I glance from him to the new judge. Donny is acting jealous. This is hilarious.

Rocker boy Donny, who's always had his pick of the girls, is jealous of me. He's always been flirty, but I never thought of his advances as anything more than typical boy behavior. Could it be that his interest in me is more than superficial?

Great, I'm so lost in thought about Donny that I missed what Theodore just said. I smile and bite my bottom lip. "Sorry, I missed that."

Theodore gives me a knowing look. "How long have you two been together?"

"Who?"

He points between Donny and me.

Oh. *Oh!*

"We actually aren't. Donny is my best friend's *much* younger brother. He just showed up at the same cabin, and then I hurt him with a skillet, so let him stay, and now my assistant broke her arm, and I needed help." Okay, that was word vomit of the worst kind. What is wrong with me?

Donny slings his arm around my shoulder. "First off, I'm not that much younger. Secondly..."

He stops talking mid-sentence and drops his arm after catching my glare.

Theodore chuckles. "I'd better head over and say hi

to Jackson Welch. It was nice meeting you both."

Jackson Welch. My arch-nemesis in the design competition and probably the best designer I've ever met.

I stick my hand out. "Nice to meet you, too."

Theodore shakes my hand on the way out. He pauses at the bottom of the steps. "For the record, I think you two look good together." He winks at me. "You should give Donny a chance."

My mouth falls open as I watch him leave, chuckling all the way.

Donny points across the room, his gaze locked on Theodore, who just disappeared up the ladder. "I like him," he declares, a faint smirk tugging at the corners of his mouth.

"Yeah, right," I retort, lifting my half-empty water bottle from the polished wooden counter, the cool condensation glistening in the afternoon sunlight. "You didn't seem to like him five minutes ago."

"That's because I thought you found him attractive," Donny shoots back, his tone playful yet defensive.

I sputter as I take a sip, spilling water down my chin. "Ew. Not at all. He's way too... old for my taste," I say, rolling my eyes dramatically.

"You seemed interested," he counters, crossing his arms and raising a brow.

"As a designer only, I like older men, but not that much older," I reply, then ask with a giggle, "You think he's attractive?"

"What? I don't check men out!" he protests, gesturing toward the door with a dismissive wave. "But he seems like one of those guys that women just... flock to, you know?"

"Like they flock to you?" I lift an eyebrow, unable to resist the jab.

"Women do not flock to me," he replies, scoffing as if the very idea is absurd.

"Liar. You forget I've been in your life for many years, and I've seen the effect you have on girls."

"Seen it or experienced it?" He steps closer, the intensity in his gaze igniting like firecrackers exploding against the night sky on the Fourth of July. I find myself laughing at the ever-present banter between us.

Before things get weirder, I slip around the small kitchen counter, which I soon realize was a mistake when Donny follows. "Seen it," I say with the confidence of a turtle trying to outrun a rabbit.

"Now who's the liar?"

With a huff, I close the distance between us. "I'm not a liar, Donny Sharp."

His grin doubles in size.

I've never been this close to Donny before. Well, at least not like this. We used to wrestle and play fight when we were kids. Back then, I never thought he was cute. It would've been odd for a twelve-year-old to be interested in a nine-year-old.

But now, he smells of mint and strawberry shampoo. And I believe I'm flirting. Ignoring that thought, I poke his chest, raising my face to his. "Did you use my shampoo?"

"I sure did. It smells good." He laughs as he leans in so close our lips are just a breath apart. I breathe in the minty scent. "Reminds me of you."

Neither of us moves for what feels like an entire minute. Finally, he raises an eyebrow. "If you don't want to be well and properly kissed right now, you'd better take a few steps back."

My back hits the stove as I shuffle away from Donny. "You're the one who needs to move out of my way. We have work to do, remember?"

He steps aside, and I glimpse his grin as I do my best

to create some distance between us.

Shawna bounces into the room. "Ooh, Jane, I thought you said you don't like Donny, but I think you lied."

Heat blooms up my neck as I stare out the small window, considering taking a page from my design assistant's book and jumping off the back of the boat. Not that I want to break my arm, but I'm not sure how I'll survive both Donny and Shawna for the next couple of weeks.

Chapter 9

Shawna hands me a bag from the bakery before moving next to Jane. "Did you lie?" she asks, trying to whisper to Jane, but her voice carries across the small space.

"No, I didn't lie. I only meant we don't like each other in a boyfriend-girlfriend type of way." Jane snatches the bag from me and pops a donut hole in her mouth before nodding at me. "Right, Donny?"

"Speak for yourself."

Jane's phone buzzes with a new message. She looks at it for a moment before groaning. "That's the director. She wants to meet with all the contestants. I'll be back as soon as I can." She hesitates at the doorway. "Donny, will you please start sanding the kitchen cabinets?"

"On it, boss lady."

"I'll help Donny," Shawna says as she pulls a jelly-filled donut out of the bag. She hands it to me and pulls out another one. "As soon as we finish our break."

"Five minutes, then back to work." Jane wags her finger at us, but the mischievous look on her face shows she's joking.

Shawna waves at Jane, drops her donut in the bag, and narrows her eyes. "Spill."

I cock my head to the left before biting a chunk of my raspberry-filled donut. After chasing it down with a swig of water, I glance at Shawna. "What do you mean? Spill what?"

"I want the truth about you and Jane. Do you like her or not?"

Oh, I guess she doesn't beat around the bush. "I've liked Jane for years, but she only likes me as a friend."

"Do you love her?"

That second bite of the donut sticks halfway down. Coughs start in my chest as I gasp for air, and I wonder if Shawna knows CPR?

She doubles up her fist and beats me on the back a few times until the donut comes up. I find myself thinking that CPR is so overrated. Nothing better than getting a lung or two bruised, but at least I'm alive. Saved from the donut.

"Are you okay, or should I get help?"

I hold my finger up as I gulp in another deep breath. "I'll be fine. Thanks. Maybe we should get to work."

Fifteen minutes later, Jane is back, and we've only sanded a partial cabinet door. She flings her hand to her hip. "Slackers."

Shawna shakes her head. "No, we are not slackers. I thought Donny was going to choke to death."

The amusement on Jane's face turns to concern. "What happened?"

Great. How am I going to win a date with Jane if she thinks I'm not even smart enough to eat a donut without choking? "A chunk of raspberry-filled donut went down the wrong pipe. I'm fine."

"Goodness. I'm glad you're okay. I remember your

mom always saying you ate too fast. Maybe she was right."

"Oh, that's not why he choked," Shawna says.

"Really?"

"Yeah, he choked when I asked him if he loves you," Shawna says casually, as if she just mentioned that my shirt is green. No big deal.

Jane grabs the neck of her Rick Springfield sweatshirt. "What would possess you to ask Donny that?"

"I wanted to know the answer. But he choked, so he never answered me. Will you tell me now, Donny?"

"Whoa, whoa, whoa." Jane's hands shoot up, palm out, like she's a cautious police officer directing traffic. "We don't need to um. To um." She scratches her ear, pulls a pink hair scrunchie from her pocket, and wraps it around her wrist. "I think we should stop for the day. It's getting late." She takes Shawna's hand and pulls her up the steps and out of sight.

I stand there, staring at the spot Jane left, my heart pounding as tremors run up my spine. That choking episode must have caused some issues.

Chapter 10

It's close to ten o'clock, and Donny is still a no-show. I can't say I blame him, especially after the pointed question Shawna directed at him earlier.

Bugs buzz around the light in the backyard. I'm thankful for the screened-in back porch. With the temperature rising, it's warm enough for mosquitoes. The last thing I want is to be bothered by their relentless buzzing and itchy bites. The screens provide a perfect barrier, allowing me to enjoy the river view without the annoyance of pesky insects.

I shift my leg underneath me and push the porch swing to sway with the cool night breeze. My eyes flick to Shawna. "I still can't believe you asked Donny if he loves me."

She blows on her hot cocoa and sips it, her face turning serious. "I told you I want to know the answer."

"But why?"

"He makes you smile, and I like that. You're beautiful when you smile."

My eyes widen, and I can't help but grin. "Am I ugly when I'm not smiling?"

"Oh, no. Are you mad at me? Did I do wrong?"

I wrap my arm around Shawna and pull her in a little closer. "No, I'm not mad at you."

"He loves you, I'm sure of it."

"There's no way. He's got a crush. Or maybe he wants to prove to himself that he can date an older woman. That must be it."

A frog belts out a song from the riverbank. Shawna stands and walks toward the door. "I'm sleepy. Goodnight, Jane."

"Goodnight. I love you."

"Love you, too," she says before disappearing inside.

I turn my attention to my computer and type in the new judge's name. The screen spins before my search results appear. I click an article from a blogger from New York.

> *Theodore Baldwin, owner and lead designer of Baldwin Home, is the host of a new design show premiering next April. I had the chance to sit down with the respected business owner for an interview. Continue reading if you want to learn what inspired him to become a designer and, most importantly, if he is single.*

I continue reading the article and find that an old friend inspired him to design, and yes, he is single.

The back door snaps shut with a resonant thud. "I thought you were sleepy," I say, my gaze fixed on the soft ripples dancing across the water's surface.

"Not at all," Donny replies, a hint of mischief in his eyes as he lowers himself onto the swing beside me, the chains creaking softly under his weight. "I'd much rather spend time out here with you."

"Oh goodness, I thought you were Shawna." I snap

my laptop closed. "Where have you been?"

"Jesse took me out on patrol with him," Donny explains, his voice filled with an excitement that brightens his demeanor. "Sorry, I should've texted you."

"No, that's fine," I say, waving my hand dismissively. "You're a big boy and don't answer to me."

"Seriously," he insists, running a hand through his tousled hair. "I should've at least told you I was coming in late. It won't happen again."

I nod, appreciating the sincerity in his eyes, wondering what the night ahead might hold for us. The answer is nothing but a quick good night, and that will be that. I need to get my head on straight.

"Okay." My gaze moves to the water. Shadows dance around the edges of the yard, creating an almost magical atmosphere. I'm very aware of Donny's arm next to mine. I scoot over until our arms are out of reach.

He chuckles. "I was waiting for you to do that."

"Do what?" I ask, my tone as innocent as a newborn rabbit's.

"Move away from me."

"So?" I elbow his side.

He grunts and catches my elbow, tugging me closer. "Jane."

His eyes shimmer like the lake. A slight aroma of mint snags my senses as we have a stare-off. "Yes?" I whisper.

"Would you and Shawna join me for dinner tomorrow night at Kristi's Kitchen in Des Arc?" His tone matches mine, low, but it has a huskiness to it that mine lacks.

Part of me wants to say yes. A big part. But I need to stop these feelings. "I would say yes, but I need to put a few finishing touches on the houseboat. Fish sounds good. I'm sure Shawna would be happy to go, but can I have a rain check?" There I go rambling again. I snatch my laptop as I bolt out of the swing. "I'd better get some sleep. Night, Donny."

"Good night, Jane." His fingers glide down my wrist, bringing a warm shiver to my skin as my fingers come to rest in his grasp. "I want to spend more time with you. Would y'all go out on the river after church with us on Sunday? Jesse invited us out on his boat."

"Yep." A breathless whisper carries the word, as if something stole the very air from my lungs. I pull my hand away, my nails digging into my palms, desperate to stop the thrill swirling in my belly. This won't do. Why am I making a big deal out of this? We'll be with a group, so there's no need to hesitate or make things weird.

Still, I hum "I Want to Know What Love Is" by Foreigner as I skip down the hall to the room I'm sharing with Shawna, a smile playing on my lips like a little girl with a secret.

Chapter 11

A slow-moving current breaks the water's surface as Jesse maneuvers his massive boat away from a bundle of dead branches floating on the river.

"Are you excited to see who makes it to the finale?" Summer, Jesse's wife, asks Jane.

Jane laid her windbreaker on the seat beside her before looking at Summer with a cute smile. "Excited and nervous."

"I still can't believe our little town has a TV show

being filmed here," Jesse adds before stopping the boat close to an old bridge. He glances toward Jane and Summer as he kills the engine. "Donny says if you don't get into the finale, he'll be shocked because you're so good."

A hot flush colors my cheeks. "I just think the houseboat looks great." Why am I blushing like an adolescent? I'm Donald Braxton Sharp, not some school-aged boy with a crush. Who am I kidding? I've had the same crush on Jane for so long that I may as well be that kid following her and Clara around.

Jane's gaze moved to mine, ensnaring me like a fish on a hook. "You said that? I think it's sweet."

"Why did you call her Chuck Norris?" Shawna asks, tugging on her borrowed pink life vest.

I hold my hand up. "Remember how she hit me with a skillet the first night I was here?"

Laughter explodes from everyone. I wait for it to die down before continuing. "Well, she reminded me of that tough-guy actor."

"Oh. I think you should call her Chuckie."

A high-pitched shriek tumbles from Jane. "Chuckie? No way."

"Why not?" Shawna cocks her head, puckering her

lips.

With a continuous shake of her head, Jane wags her pointer finger at Shawna. "Because all I can think about is the killer doll with the same name."

I wink at Shawna before turning to Jane with a wicked smile. "Then I agree with Shawna. Chuckie is a fitting nickname."

For a moment, Jane and I stare at one another, our eyes engaging in a battle I can't quite describe. And why is my heart feeling this weird sensation?

"Can we go fishing like the man over there?" Shawna asks, interrupting my moment with Jane.

"I think that can be arranged," I say to Shawna, but my eyes stay on Jane. "If Jane says it's okay."

Jane takes a swig of her water. "That'll be fine. I mean, if we find the time. But I guess we can make the time."

A big splash interrupts my thoughts. I open my eyes in time to see Shawna's head disappear into the murky water.

Chapter 12

I scramble to the side of the boat and climb onto it. In the split second before I jump, Donny dives into the water with Jesse right behind him.

Summer takes hold of my arm, helping me down. I'd only get in their way. Tears stream down my face as my gaze lands on the discarded life vest Shawna had been wearing. How did she manage to get it off without my noticing? This is all my fault.

After what seems like a full minute, Jesse's head

emerges a few feet from the boat. My fingernails bite into the tender skin of my palm. "Where is Shawna?"

Donny breaks through the water, Shawna clinging to his side. Jesse and Donny flank her, guiding her to the boat's ladder.

She climbs onto the deck, her gaze lowered. Summer drapes a blanket around Shawna's shoulders. "I'm sorry. Are you mad at me, Chuckie?"

I open my mouth only to snap it shut, biting my lip to keep from laughing at the new and very much unwanted nickname Shawna has given me. "I'm not mad at you. Why did you do it?"

"I've always wanted to jump out of a boat, but Daddy and Mom wouldn't let me. They don't think I can do anything."

My heart softens a little as I imagine what Shawna goes through. She has a high-functioning level of autism, but she tries not to let that define her. Even though my aunt and uncle are overprotective, Shawna works hard to be her own person and make her own decisions. I wrap my arm around her. "They trusted you enough to come here with me."

Her face brightens, and she shivers. "They sure did. I'm still really sorry, but it was so fun I'd like to do it again."

"Oh no, you don't. At least not right now," I say, handing the life vest to Shawna.

Later that evening, I bring three mugs of cocoa outside. Donny turns from the white screen. "Okay, Shawna, fire up the projector."

Clara squeals from the laptop screen. "Archer and I can't wait to watch Pride and Prejudice with y'all."

Not one to break tradition, I sink onto the fluffy outdoor sectional. "How many more times do we have to watch it before we reach your goal?"

Clara leans into the screen. "Our goal, Jane. I distinctly remember you and me both deciding to watch it a hundred times before we're thirty."

"I know, I know. How old were we? Like fourteen?"

"Nope, we were sixteen. And just for that, I'm not telling you how many times."

Archer Banks, the famous football player who happens to be my best friend's husband, snatches the folder from Clara's hand. "Based on this spreadsheet, you have twenty-two times to watch it before meeting the goal of a hundred."

Yes, Clara has an ongoing spreadsheet to track our progress toward our goal. Listen, I have nothing against Pride and Prejudice. It's a great book and a wonderful movie. I'm even named after the very Jane Bennet from the book. My mom just so happens to have the last name Bennett, and she loves Jane Austen. So when she got pregnant as a teenager, she named me after her favorite writer and character.

Clara snatches the folder away. Then, she gazes straight into the camera with a look that scares me. "Hey, Donny, sit by Jane to keep her warm."

I literally choke on my own spit.

Donny chooses that moment to listen to his sister. He plops down beside me, draping his arm across my shoulder. "Sure thing, sis."

I wiggle out of his grasp. My heart slams into my ribs as tingling overtakes my entire body.

Clara smirks.

Thank goodness, the one who kick-started Clara's love for all things Jane Austen walks into the back-yard. The glow of the outdoor light illuminates Mom's face. Her blonde hair cascades down her back, and I'm convinced she looks younger than I do.

"What's going on out here? Did I make it in time to join the party?"

A grin stretches across my face as I watch the woman I admire the most climb the steps. Not only did she finish college pregnant, but she also started a design business and raised me with only a little help from her brother. My grandparents both passed away when I was a baby, leaving Mom to fend for herself and me before she reached twenty.

I unlatch the screen door. "Come on up, Mom. The more the merrier," I say as she squeezes me in a tight hug, and all is right in the world.

Chapter 13

The following morning, Mom pulls into the basin parking lot and stops in front of the massive tent. Today is the day we find out who makes it to the finale. She clears her throat. "Did you hear me?"

I rub the back of my neck, take a breath, and will my heart rate to slow down. It's no use. "I'm sorry, Mom. What did you say?"

Shawna leans forward, her hand wrapped around the back of my headrest. "She said don't be nervous.

You'll be in the top two!"

My breath hitches, a prickle crawling up my spine as I expel the air, bracing for the day. Normally, it doesn't bother me when she gets loud, but today my stomach clenches up like a roly-poly hiding from a predator. I wag my head with a slight smile.

"I agree," Donny says from the seat beside Shawna.

For the past few days, I've focused on putting the finishing touches on the houseboat, so I've been able to push the results out of my mind. Right now, I can think of nothing else.

"Hey, Jane," Shawna says, "it's okay if you don't win. I still think you are the best designer in the world."

Mom turns an amused expression toward Shawna. "Oh, is that right? I thought I was your favorite designer."

"Oh, no, you're not," Shawna grins. "But you are my favorite aunt."

With a shocked expression, Mom throws her hand over her heart. "Well, I guess that's better than nothing."

No longer able to fight my smile, my lips edge up at the corners. I open the door and step out. "Let's get this over with."

Donny hops out, stopping beside me. "That's the spirit," he says, pulling me close for a hug.

The show's host and a cameraman stop a few feet away. Donny takes a step back toward Mom, leaving my entire right side chilled.

"Welcome to Small Town, Big Design! I'm Walter Jenkins, and we're live from the charming town of DeValls Bluff, Arkansas! The anticipation is electric as the contestants arrive, ready to find out who will secure a spot in the finale. Their fate hangs in the balance! Joining us now is our viewers' favorite from the last competition, the incredibly talented Jane Bennett! Good morning, Jane! How are you feeling as we gear up for the big results?"

With a flash of my brightest smile, I meet Donny's gaze. "I have to admit, I'm feeling nervous. I understand how talented the other contestants are, and I know that must make things difficult for the judges."

"Speaking of judges, here comes Theodore Baldwin, the guest judge for the finale."

Theodore stops next to the host, a broad smile on his face. "Good morning!"

"Theodore's new show, Design by Theo, will premiere next month, generating a wave of excitement not only among the contestants vying for the spotlight on Small Town, Big Design but also among our dedicated viewers who have eagerly anticipated this moment."

With a subtle twist of his body, Theodore turns to face me, but his gaze darts to a point just behind me. The color drains from his face as he inhales deeply, a mixture of disbelief and shock etched across his features.

"Theo?" Mom's voice emerges as a choked whisper, thick with shock and disbelief.

His eyes widen further. "Abby?"

A cold wave washes over me, contrasting with the heat of the moment. My heart races, feeling the weight of the tension in the air.

Seeing the drama unfold, the host gestures for the cameraman to pivot, capturing the raw emotion of the scene.

Mom's breath catches, and tears spill down her cheeks as she sobs, "I can't believe it's you."

Theodore steps closer, narrowing the gap between them, his hands outstretched as if he's almost afraid to make contact. He peers into her eyes, his voice filled with emotion as he asks, "Do you know how long I searched for you?"

What is even happening here? My stomach churns, and I fight the rising nausea threatening to overtake me. The air is somehow thicker with tension as Donny hands Mom a tissue, his eyes darting between us. She takes it, her gaze fixed intently on the new guest judge. "I tried to find you," she murmurs, her voice barely above a whisper.

"Are you here for me?" he asks, his tone laced with curiosity and a hint of something deeper.

Mom shakes her head, her eyes flickering to me, a silent message passing between us. "No, not for you," she replies.

"Then why?" he presses, his expression shifting as he follows her gaze, a mix of confusion and concern etched on his face.

I can't hold back any longer. "What's going on here?" I demand, moving my eyes from her to him, searching for answers. "How do you know Theodore, Mom?"

His head swivels towards me, and we lock eyes for a moment that feels electric. "Did you just call Abby Mom?" he asks, his surprise clear as he processes my question.

"Yeah, why? How do you know each other?" I narrow my eyes as my pulse quickens.

Mom wraps her trembling hand around my wrist, the contact sending a shiver up my spine. "Can we go somewhere private?"

This is getting weird, and an icy clench of dread settles in my stomach. Whatever is happening can't be good, and the tension in the air is suffocating me.

The cameraman lowers his camera, sensing the shift in our conversation. Theodore runs a hand down his face. "Is Jane my daughter?" he asks, a host of emotions playing out in his expression.

Mom nods. That was not a denial. It's a definitive yes that reveals more than words ever could.

In that moment, reality sinks in like a stone. Theodore Baldwin is my father.

Chapter 14

I snatch the keys from Mom's hand and bolt to my Jeep. Mom calls my name, but I can't deal with her right now. My hands shake as I insert the key in the ignition and slam it into reverse. Gravel pings the Toyota Camry beside me as I peel out of the parking lot.

Destination: I have no idea.

I don't even know why I'm leaving. From the looks of it, Theodore did not know he had a kid. Why had I never asked for his name? Why had Mom never told me more about him? About what happened? The only thing she's said is that I came about when she was going through a hard time, and they lost touch. She calls me her little light since I supposedly helped her out of a dark place. But how did they lose touch?

Theodore doesn't even look old enough to have a kid my age. I gasp. Is that why Mom never talked about him? Was she involved with a minor? My mind whirls with what ifs.

I pull over in front of Craig's BBQ and zip around. I'm not the one who needs to give answers, so why am I the one running away? I'm not a coward, nor am I one to run away when things get tough.

There's also the matter of the competition. I glance at the clock. The live show to air the results I've been waiting for starts in an hour. It's time for me to grow up and face my problems head-on. And who knows if I'm running away from more than the situation. Maybe I'm running from the competition. My nerves. My anxiety. Donny Sharp.

That's a load of bull. I have no reason to run from Donny Sharp. There's nothing between us but a bit of attraction. I bet if I kissed him, then that would be the end of the so-called zing I've been feeling.

Dust kicks up when a red convertible Mustang slides to a stop beside me. The dark-haired girl in the driver's seat meets my gaze and waves. "I can't believe this! You're Jane Bennett!" she says, tucking a few dark hairs into her black ball cap.

I roll the window down a few more inches. "Yeah," I say, squirming in my seat, not used to people recognizing me.

"My mom and I want you to win so badly," the girl continues. "My name is Genny, by the way."

A blonde girl with striking blue eyes leans forward, her expression sharp and incredulous as she snaps a dirty look at Genny. "Do you really know Donny Sharp?"

"I mean, we grew up together. What would make you ask that?" I ask, creeper vibes hitting me hard.

The blonde girl shrugs, a coy smile snaking onto her lips. "Oh, I saw a post online about someone spotting you two together in town. I just think it's cool, you know? I think he's a hot singer."

A black Chevy sedan pulls into the parking lot with Mom hanging out the passenger window. Good grief.

By the time they pull in, Mom is out of the car.

Donny waves from the driver's seat but makes no move to get out.

Genny pulls her ball cap closer as she backs out, zooming away toward Hazen. I guess they were just nosy teenagers after all. They didn't even notice Donny driving the car.

Mom beelines it to me. "Jane, sweetheart, I'm so sorry."

I hop out, holding my hands up. "No, we're not doing this. I don't need apologies. I want to know what happened. Every detail."

With a sigh, Mom's eyes dart around the parking lot. "Can we go somewhere more private?"

"No." I do my best to remain firm, but it's hard with the way my throat is achingly thick.

"How about I give you the shorter version, then we finish our conversation at the cabin this afternoon?" She glances at her watch. "Since you need to be ready for the results in less than an hour."

"Fine."

"I was introduced to Theo when I was a junior, and he was a freshman in college." She pauses and takes a deep breath. "Honestly, Jane, I hate to relive this time in my life. I wasn't the person God would have me be, and I'm ashamed of how I behaved."

She takes a step toward me, wrapping my hands in hers. Her eyes brim with tears. "I absolutely do not regret having you. Please don't misunderstand what I'm saying. You are the best thing that has ever happened to me. You caused me to see things differently. I no longer cared only about myself. It was you. My shining bright light."

Tears pooled in my eyes as I clung to Mom's hands. My lifeline. The person I've always looked up to. The one who has always been there for me, no matter what. I realize that I'm not the only one hurting here. There are three of us. "I love you so much, Mom, and I promise you I could never think poorly of you. I mean, who doesn't have a past they're ashamed of? Or at least things they regret? I understand."

"Theo and a group of his friends came to Conway for a ballgame. Theo was so good-looking, with tousled hair and warm, inviting eyes that sparkled. We both found ourselves swept up in a whirlwind of attraction, indulging in reckless fun that felt exhilarating at the moment. By the end of the night, I had his name and number written on a crumpled piece of paper that I tucked away in my purse, promising I would call him soon."

"Why didn't you make that call?" I ask, genuine curiosity etched on my face.

"I lost my purse," Mom admits, frustration creeping into her voice. "All I could recall was that his name was Theo, and he lived somewhere in Fayetteville. Can you imagine how many people named Theo lived in that city?"

"You didn't get his last name?" I press.

"Nope," Mom sighs. "His last name was scribbled on that piece of paper, now long gone, leaving me with only the faint hope of somehow finding him again."

My phone buzzes with an incoming text. I glance down and blow my lips. "It's Lisa Flowers, the director."

We need you here ASAP.

"She needs me there. Can we finish this talk afterwards?"

"Absolutely, baby girl."

Chapter 15

By the time we make it back to the tent, Theodore Baldwin is nowhere to be seen.

Lisa Flowers speed-walks over to me. Her eyes dart to Mom and then back to me. "I can't say I've ever had something so interesting happen during a live recording."

Mom inclines her head toward Lisa. "I'm so sorry. I hope what happened didn't cause too much trouble."

"Oh no, of course not. If anything, it boosted our

ratings. More people have tuned in since...the incident."

Great. Of all the times I daydreamed of the moment I met my father, never once did it happen on live television.

"Thanks for letting us borrow your car," Mom says, her eyes on the cameraman.

"Anytime." He takes a step closer, his gaze penetrating hers. "I mean that."

"Okay, we should probably get ready." I take Mom's hand.

Once we're out of earshot, she sighs. "Thanks for getting me out of that. I think he was going to ask me out."

"Of course he was. You look like you're a thirty-year-old model, not a forty-four-year-old mom."

"Ha ha. No matter. Right now my focus is on you and figuring out how to make this right."

"Seriously, you don't have to make anything right. I understand. You always told me you lost contact with my father before he knew you were pregnant, so it's not like you lied."

"I love you so much." Mom kisses me on the cheek, pulling me close.

"Love you, too." I hug her back. "Now, make yourself useful and help me fix my makeup."

Less than an hour later, the moment arrives. I stand on stage with the other contestants, waiting for the results.

The host glances at the card in his hand. "The first contestant making it to the finale is..." He pauses, looking at each contestant. "Jackson Welch!"

Jackson fist pumps before waving at the audience.

The host flashes a dazzling smile at the camera. "We have two designers left and only one spot in the finale. Judge Trixie, what did you find to be the most difficult challenge in picking your favorite houseboat design?"

Trixie Spencer takes a slow sip from her insulated cup. "Honestly, I've had my top pick since the first episode, and I struggled to look at the design and designer separately."

What in the world does that even mean?

The host's smile flickers for a moment. Apparently, he didn't understand either. "Great. Thanks for that." He glances at the card in his hand before turning to the stage. "This was a close one. These contestants gave their all, as you've all seen over the past few weeks. Without further ado, the final contestant to make it to the finale is... Jane Bennett!"

Did he say I made it to the finale? This must be a dream. My heart may catapult out of my chest.

Donny screams my name like I'm a senior in high school walking across the stage to receive my diploma. I would be embarrassed, but right now, all I feel is thankful. A bubbly sensation overtakes my heart as I throw my arms in the air.

"Stay tuned to the next episode as we explore fixing up a historical landmark right here in DeValls Bluff. Yes, that's right, each contestant will have a part of the closed-down Castleberry Hotel to redesign."

After a few interviews and a lot of congratulations, my body is so ready to get some rest. The smile that I thought was fixed to my face drops when we pull into the driveway at the cabin.

Theodore Baldwin waves from where he's leaning on a white Mercedes.

Chapter 16

Mom jumps out of the Jeep faster than a deer sprints onto the highway from the woods. Theodore walks toward her. They stare at one another for a second before embracing.

Donny squeezes my shoulder from the back seat. "You gonna talk to him?"

"I think you should," Shawna says. "You've always wanted to know your daddy."

She's not wrong.

"From what it sounds like, he didn't know about you." Donny removes his hand, leaving me feeling like I lost something.

Get a grip, Jane.

"I know he didn't," I say before climbing out of the Jeep.

Theodore drapes his hands across Mom's shoulders. "I am in shock," he says.

Yeah, that makes two of us. I stick my hand out, like we are in a business meeting. "I guess we should start over. Hi, I'm Jane Bennett, the long-lost daughter you never knew you had."

"Hi, Jane." He takes my hand in his. "I'd rather have a hug, if that's okay with you."

I meet Theodore's questioning look. He has my eyes. Or rather, I have his. My stomach pitches as I step into his arms.

I'm hugging my dad.

My *dad*.

His chest tightens as he holds me close. "This is unreal. Abby, we have a daughter." He leans back and meets my gaze. "You look so much like my sister."

Mom rests her hand on my back. "Should we go inside and talk?"

"That's probably a good idea. Just give me a second."
I back away from Theodore and motion toward Donny and Shawna.

Donny rolls the window down. "Hey, Shawna, do you want to go to Craig's BBQ?"

"Yes, please."

"Thank you," I say, my steps light as I walk toward my mom. And my dad. I never thought I'd be able to say those words.

Once inside, Mom plays hostess by pouring three glasses of sweet tea. I take a sip of mine and set it on the table. Mom and I settle onto the sofa while Theodore takes a seat on the swivel recliner.

"Jane already knows we met at a party when I was a junior, and you were a freshman in college."

A red flush covers Theo's cheeks. He swallows and turns to Mom. "Abby, I can't tell you how sorry I am."

"I'm the one who lost your number," Mom says, her voice laced with regret.

"I know," he replies, his tone heavy, "but I have to confess something that you won't like at all."

A deep crease forms between Mom's brows as she exchanges a concerned glance with me. "What do you mean?"

"Remember when I told you I was a freshman in college?" Theo's voice wavers.

"Yeah, you said you were studying in Fayetteville," Mom says, her brow still furrowed in confusion as she leans forward.

Taking a deep breath, he rubs the back of his neck. "I wasn't quite in college when we met. Abby, I was still a senior in high school."

Mom shoots up from the couch with such suddenness that it lurches backward, the cushions shifting beneath her. "What?"

Theo stands, the tension clear in his rigid stance as he tries to steady his resolve. "But I was eighteen," he adds quickly.

"That doesn't make it any better," she replies sharply, disappointment etched on her face, her voice trembling with mixed emotions. "But I guess it doesn't matter at this point."

"Please forgive me. I was young and stupid, and honestly, I fell in love with you the moment our eyes met. You filled my mind and my heart. My friends thought I was off my rocker, but I didn't care."

"Why didn't you find me?"

"Trust me, I tried. I even hired a private investigator

once I started earning money, but every Abby or Abigail who attended college in Conway the year we met was not you."

Mom's laughter sprinkles the air.

Theodore and I exchange a glance before she continues. "I didn't go to college in Conway. I went to Harding University in Searcy."

"I always wondered why you didn't call me. After the private investigator struck out, I just figured what I felt was one-sided."

"Not at all. I bet I put ten thousand miles on my little Toyota Camry driving to Fayetteville searching for you."

"I can't believe it. We have a daughter. This is just. Wow." He turns to me. "Tell me about yourself. I want to know everything."

My mind shifts as I blink to clear my thoughts. What a story. I always pictured myself jumping into my father's arms when we met for the first time. Now that I finally have the opportunity, why is my stomach churning with dread?

Chapter 17

A warm orange glow spills from the bedroom window as the sun's golden edge begins to break through the swirling, vibrant clouds. The rich aroma of freshly brewed coffee wafts through the air, teasing my senses and igniting my desire to rise. Yet, I remain anchored to the bed, mesmerized by the breathtaking scene outside, my mind lost in the overwhelming encounter with my biological father.

I can't believe it's been three days since we met. It

didn't unfold the way I've always thought it would. He had no clue about my existence, and I can't hold that against him.

Mom always told me she lost contact with my father after a brief, tumultuous relationship and that, despite her efforts, she was unable to locate him. There were moments when I thought she might have made that story up to shield me from the truth. But now, faced with the reality of what happened, it doesn't erase the years of longing for a father figure in my life.

Theodore strikes me as kind-hearted, and his genuine desire to get to know me is evident in the way he looked at me after finding out who I am. Still, after witnessing the way he reacted to seeing Mom, I can't shake the unsettling feeling that he might be more interested in rekindling something with her than in forming a bond with me.

As I pick up a granola bar, Mom's voice filters through the closed door, her tone tinged with worry. "Jane? Are you awake yet?"

My gaze lands on a still sleeping Shawna before tiptoeing to the door. "I'm awake, Mom."

Shawna glances up with bloodshot eyes. "Is it time to get up?"

"No, it's early. I'm gonna go talk to Mom," I say as I slip into my pink fuzzy slippers.

With a thumbs up, Shawna throws a leg out of the cover before dozing back off.

As soon as I close the door behind me, Mom pulls me into a tight hug. Tears sting my eyes as a surge of heaviness wells up inside my chest.

Mom runs a hand down the back of my head, comforting me like I'm a child. "It's okay, baby. I promise."

Moisture spills through my lashes, and I give in to the sobs threatening to overtake me. My dreams of meeting my father are a reality. Why am I crying over this? With a pinch of my lips, I stomp my foot. "I'm okay. Just overwhelmed, I guess."

Mom cups my cheeks in her hands, her touch warm and grounding. "Meeting Theo like this has to be emotionally draining. I know my mind is all jumbled, so I can hardly imagine what yours must be like. It must feel like a storm of confusion and conflicting emotions."

"I don't understand why I feel angry," I confess, my voice barely above a whisper.

"At me?" she asks, her brow furrowing. "I understand how you feel. I feel the same way. I'm angry at myself for losing his number and upset that both you and he have missed out on so much time together. But amid that anger, there's also a flicker of gratitude and hope for the future. I pray that the two of you can connect and form the bond that was meant to be." As she speaks, tears well up in the corners of her eyes.

"I love you, Mom."

"I love you, too, baby."

The heaviness in my chest lifts. I'm a grown woman, more than able to deal with a few life changes. My lips quirk into a grin. "Not to change the subject, but I need coffee."

Mom links her arm with mine, leading me toward the kitchen. "I don't want to pressure you, but I heard there's an amazing country cooking café in Des Arc. How would you feel about meeting Theo there for breakfast?"

"By myself?" I stop in my tracks.

Mom stops in front of the coffee maker. "It would give you an opportunity to get to know him better," she says as she pours the rich, dark liquid into a simple, ceramic mug

"Okay, but let me at least drink a cup of coffee before I leave," I reply, trying to gather my thoughts.

Mom hands me the steaming cup, and I cradle it, savoring the familiar aroma that always feels like home. I blow gently on the coffee's surface, letting the warmth envelop me. "What's the name of the restaurant?"

"TJ's Country Kitchen."

Chapter 18

With a bar covering almost the entire right side of the café, booths along the other wall, and tables in the center of the room, TJ's Country Kitchen gives off old-school, homemade, down-home cooking vibes. And I love it. The sweet scent of syrup and butter coats my tongue before the door has time to close behind me.

Our server, a thin woman with a kind smile, lays two menus on the table. "Morning, folks. I'll be back in just a minute to take your orders."

After we get our food, a few moments of awkward silence hang between us. Finally, Theodore pushes a piece of bacon around his plate before clearing his throat and meeting my gaze head-on. "I know this has to be weird for you, but I need you to know I'm so happy to have an opportunity to know you."

The syrupy pancake bite clogs my throat. I drop my gaze to my cup and take a gulp of lukewarm coffee. "I mean, it's definitely not something I planned on doing while also navigating a design competition."

"Yeah, I don't know about you, but I feel a little exposed after our meeting aired on live television."

I pinch my fingers together and grin. "Just a tad."

He sets his fork down and leans against the wooden booth. "Tell me about kindergarten."

"Kindergarten? Why?"

Our server stops by our table. "Can I get you any-thing else?"

I hold my coffee cup out. She tops it off before moving to the next table.

Theodore shrugs and closes his eyes. "I missed it. I'd ask you about preschool, but I'm not sure you'll remember that far back."

"Oh. Well, I do remember preschool. That's when I met my best friend, Clara."

"Isn't she Donny's sister?" he asks before finishing off his toast.

"That's right." Maybe he has been paying attention. As some of the tension eases from my shoulders, I tell him all I can remember about kindergarten and preschool.

"Will you send me pictures?" He rests his hand on the table, his fingers folding the napkin over and over. "I'd love to see what you looked like."

"I can do that."

Both our phones buzz at the same time. Theodore's forehead creases. "It's a group text. The producer wants to meet with us in an hour."

And with that, all the delicious food I just ate sours in my stomach.

An hour later, we sit across from Martha Meadows, the producer who wastes no time upending my world. "Jane, I just got off the phone with the network. I'm sorry, but you're off the show."

I spring to stand, my heart sprinting up my throat. "What do you mean I'm off the show?"

Even though I've always gotten the impression she is a no-nonsense woman who lacks empathy, her face betrays her concern. She removes her designer red glasses and meets my panicked gaze. "I'm truly sorry, but if Theodore Baldwin is your biological father, there is a conflict. The network wants him as a judge, so we're left with no other choice but to cut you loose."

Theodore shakes his head, his expression hardening as he meets Martha's gaze. "Martha, this simply won't do."

Martha crosses her arms, her frustration evident. "Theodore, I have been going back and forth with them for three solid days, ironing out every detail, pleading Jane's case. I truly believe this will create an exciting pull for our viewers. They're eager to be immersed in the lives of our designers, to see behind the curtain of creativity. This opportunity is perfect for showcasing their struggles and triumphs, in my opinion."

The air in the room crackles with tension as I watch Theodore Baldwin, my father, try to stand up for me.

But somehow, his actions are overshadowed by the fire pulsing through my veins.

Chapter 19

Long after everyone else is asleep, my mind is at a rock concert where the singer is screaming out words no one understands. Like a fool, I thought meeting my dad would be the start of something good.

Not the end of the design competition I worked so hard to be a part of. I never dreamed I'd get kicked off the show for a conflict of interest. Never.

After finding out I was canned, I excused myself

and refused to leave my room. Yeah, I'm really mature. Shawna only came to the room at eleven, which is way past her usual bedtime. Shame pounds at my already full mind.

I wish Clara were here. All my life, I've been the girl without a dad. The one not enough to have two parents. Clara never made me feel that way. How I hate she moved to Las Vegas. If only Archer would quit football and move back to Arkansas, I'd have something to look forward to. I ache to call her, but who knows how a pregnant woman would react to getting woken up in the middle of the night? Not a good idea.

By the time a sliver of dawn cuts into the night sky, I put on a pair of Chic Jeans and an oversized Jackson Five hoodie, slip into Nike sneakers, and head out the front door. Destination: Lisa Flowers' rental house in Hazen.

Fifteen minutes later, I pull onto the gravel driveway of a charming white cottage, its front yard dotted with vibrant rose bushes that sway gently in the breeze. The morning sun casts a warm glow as I step out of my Jeep, just in time to see Lisa sprinting toward me, concern etched across her features. She skids to a halt by my vehicle, her breath coming in shallow gasps. With a swift motion, she tugs off her oversized headset and bends forward, placing her hands on her knees as she tries to regain her composure.

"I almost wish I'd taken a different route," she quips, managing a teasing smile, but the tightness around her eyes tells me she's dreading this discussion as much as I am.

I snort in frustration, the irritation lacing my words unmistakable. "The network disqualifying me over something completely beyond my control isn't just unfair, it's downright infuriating."

A frown deepens the lines around her mouth. "I hope you're smart enough to realize this wasn't my decision."

"I know that, Lisa, but you have the influence to change the outcome." My hands clench into tight fists at my sides, my mind racing with what I should say next to win Lisa over to my side. "I will do anything just to make things right."

She waves a dismissive hand in the air, a single clear jewel on each of her long fingers catching the light. "You give me more credit than you should. My influence only goes so far in this cutthroat industry."

"Will you at least talk to the network or the producer?" I plead, my voice tinged with frustration. "I should not be the one getting booted off the show. Theodore Baldwin should."

"That's your opinion," she replies coolly, her expression remaining inscrutable.

"Please, Lisa. Can't Theodore judge another show? Why does it have to be this one?" My heart races, hope flickering in my chest like a candle in front of an air conditioner vent.

When her posture deflates, a subtle but telling change, I sigh in relief.

"I'll talk to Martha Meadows and see what can be done," she concedes, her voice softening.

"Thank you, Lisa." I offer a small smile.

"Hey, don't get your hopes up," she warns, a hint of caution in her tone. "But I'll at least try."

I nod, afraid that the tears brimming in my eyes will spill over if I say anything more.

"I'll call you later, Jane," she adds, her gaze turning thoughtful. "In the meantime, get to know your father. He's a good guy."

Chapter 20

By the time I return to the cabin, Donny is standing beside the riverbank, his silhouette framed against the golden hue of the bright sun. As I step out of my Jeep, the wind carries the faint sound of water lapping against the shore. I walk down the well-worn path, my sneakers rustling through the freshly mowed grass until I reach him. "Hey," I call out.

A wave of relief washes over Donny's face, his tension visibly lifting. "Hey, Jane. I was wondering where you went." He shifts his weight from one foot to the other, eyes scanning the river as if it holds answers.

I kick a small piece of driftwood into the flowing water, watching it disappear into the swirling depths. Turning to Donny, I exhale. "I went to see the director, Lisa Flowers. I was hoping to get her help in convincing the network they've made a mistake with my project."

"How did it go?" His brows furrow, and I can see hope flickering in his eyes.

"I at least got her to agree to plead my case. It's a start," I reply, my tone more optimistic than I feel.

"So, what's next?" He shifts closer.

"I wait," I say, a hint of frustration creeping into my voice. The uncertainty gnaws at me.

"How about we go fishing while we wait?" Donny suggests.

"I don't know that I like to fish," I admit. The thought of sitting still for too long doesn't appeal to me.

"And you'll never know if you don't try," he counters, a playful grin spreading across his face. "What do you say?"

"What about Mom and Shawna?" I ask, glancing

over my shoulder toward the cabin.

"They can come too," he assures, shrugging it off.

"Okay then," I concede, intrigued despite myself.

An hour later, Donny and I climb into his friend Jesse's boat. It rocks gently with our movements. Mom and Shawna opted for a shopping trip in Stuttgart, leaving just the two of us to enjoy the adventure on the water.

After getting settled and strapping on our life vests, Donny cranks the motor with his uninjured hand. The engine roars to life, cutting through the stillness, and we zip off against the current.

Fishing with Donny turns out to be exactly what I need to clear my mind from the chaos of recent events. The rhythmic movement of my fishing bob in the water captures my full attention, and I find myself willing a fish to take the bait, almost as if my concentration could magically attract a catch.

Am I happy to meet my father after all these years without him? Yes, there's a warmth in that thought, but it's overshadowed by the frustration of being kicked off the show I've poured my heart into for so long. That disappointment feels heavy, like a stone in my stomach, making it hard to breathe deeply and enjoy the moment.

Almost as if the fish listened to me, my bob dips beneath the surface. Adrenaline floods my veins as I reel in my line. Donny shifts closer to me, and the small boat rocks gently with the waves, his excitement palpable as he leans forward. With a shout, I pull in a sizeable fish.

"Look out, Jane, you've caught a striped bass!" he exclaims, his voice a mix of surprise and pride.

"This is great!" I reply, a genuine grin spreading across my face as the shimmering fish breaks the surface, glistening in the afternoon sun like a treasure from the depths. The thrill of the catch momentarily lifts the weight of my worries, and I relish this simple triumph on the water.

"Three more and we'll have enough for dinner. You know how to clean fish?"

"What? Ew, no." I scrunch my lips together. "But I guess I can learn how."

Donny's laughter echoes down the winding river. "I got you this time, but you can clean them next time.

Deal?"

I stick my hand out. "Deal."

Chapter 21

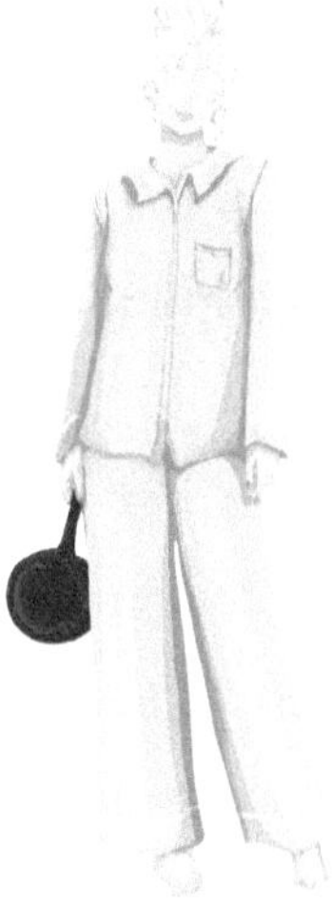

After a delectable dinner of perfectly seasoned fried fish, golden hushpuppies, and crispy fries, I lean back in my chair, fully satisfied. The rich, smoky flavors linger on my taste buds, and I can't help but smile at the comforting aroma still wafting from the kitchen. Jesse and Summer came over, and Jesse cleaned the fish to keep Donny's hand from getting infected.

Mom had suggested inviting Theodore, but the

thought of facing him sends a flutter of anxiety through me. I know I should reach out to him eventually, maybe when I feel a little less upset about the situation.

Casting my gaze out the window, I witness a heartwarming scene. Donny and Shawna are tossing a football back and forth across the lawn. The way Donny teases her as he throws a spiral makes my heart swell. He is so good to her.

Just then, Mom pops her head into my room, her expression a mix of concern and encouragement. "Hey, honey. Lisa is here to see you," she announces, nodding toward the living room.

I take a deep breath, feeling the weight of the moment as I recognize that it's time to face the music. Mom glances at me and the doorway, her protective instincts evident. "I'll be right in here if you need me," she reassures me quietly.

"Thanks, Mom," I reply, forcing a small smile as I brace myself.

Lisa wastes no time in getting to the point. "Look, Jane, I tried my best to advocate for you with the network. I really did," she begins, her tone sincere. "But they see the conflict as too great to overcome. I'm so sorry, but their final answer was no." The disappointment in her voice echoes my own feelings.

The urge to scream and throw a tantrum like a petulant two-year-old bubbles just beneath the surface. But I know that won't resolve anything. Instead, I nod slowly, forcing my voice to remain steady. "Thank you for trying, Lisa. I still don't agree with their decision, but I appreciate your effort on my behalf."

"I truly wish you the best, Jane," Lisa says, her expression softening as she squeezes my hand gently, an unspoken bond of understanding passing between us before she turns to leave. The door clicks shut behind her, leaving me alone with my swirling thoughts and a heavy heart.

Early the next morning, my mind is tangled in a chaotic bundle of knots. As the golden rays of dawn begin to creep through the window, I finally surrender to the realization that I can no longer toss and turn in bed. I spring up from the tangled sheets, the stars still twinkling faintly in the crisp morning sky, reminding me of the restless night I've endured. I need to escape this cabin, to breathe fresh air and clear my head from the weight of my thoughts.

Rushing through the room, I quickly pull on my favorite worn jeans and a soft, faded T-shirt with a roller skate design on the front. I toss a few essentials into my overnight bag, determined to focus on something beyond my racing mind.

Once in the kitchen, the faint smell of fish from last night's dinner and the early morning silence settle around me. I reach for a pen to jot down a note to Mom, asking her to bring Shawna home. As I fumble in the drawer, I find a pen that looks promising, but when I put it on the paper, nothing happens. I glance at it with mild frustration and give it a gentle shake, murmuring, "Please, won't you just work for me?"

Remarkably, the pen responds, and the ink flows smoothly as I scrawl the note. Satisfied, I fold it neatly and leave it on the counter. With one last glance around the cabin, I slip out the door, my heart racing with anticipation, and hop into my Jeep. I start the engine, feeling the familiar rumble beneath me as I pull away, blinking back tears. How could they take everything away after I was voted into the finale? Is that even legal?

My heart tightens as I continue driving, my mind buzzing with thoughts about how to fix the situation I've found myself in.

I take the exit off the interstate and roll into a small town called Brinkley, where the familiar neon sign of the Waffle House beckons me with the promise of comfort food. The aroma of frying bacon and fresh coffee fills the air as I step inside. After indulging in three steaming cups of rich black coffee and a plate of fried eggs and waffles, I feel more like myself.

As I continue my journey toward Jonesboro, my phone suddenly vibrates in my pocket. I glance at the screen and sigh with relief when I see that it's Clara and not Mom.

"Hey," I answer, trying to keep my tone casual.

"What in the world is going on, and why have you not called me?" Clara's voice crackles with a mix of concern and frustration.

"I was going to but..." I falter, searching for the right words.

"I am so mad I could bite a nail in two! You met your father, and I had to hear about it from my brother?" Her voice rises, and I can picture the crease between her eyes.

"I'm sorry, it happened so fast, and then it was so late, and I didn't want to chance calling my pregnant best friend so late. And then yesterday I talked to the director and then went fishing, and I just got so sidetracked."

"That's no excuse. I'm flying to Arkansas first thing in the morning. I have a doctor's appointment today, or I'd be on the way right now."

"You don't have to do that. My emotional breakdown will pass."

"I know I don't have to, but you are my very best friend, and I will not leave you alone to handle your, um, emotional breakdown as you call it."

"Thank you."

"Where are you headed?"

"I'm not sure. Honestly, I don't even know why I'm leaving. I just need some time away from everything so I can think through my next steps."

"Why don't you go to Tammy's in Pocahontas? I'll let her know you're coming."

"That sounds good. I'm so glad I chose you as my best friend all those years ago."

"Girl, same. Now, tell me everything."

Chapter 22

After a quick prayer, I knock on Jane's bedroom door. It hurt me last night that she went to bed upset after Lisa Flowers left. I need to tell her I'm here for her.

The doorknob slowly turns. For two heartbeats, I consider bolting down the hallway. No, if I can get up in front of thousands of people and sing, then I can tell Jane I care about her.

I gulp through a dry patch in my throat when the

door opens. The tension eases from my body when I meet Shawna's sleepy gaze. "Hey. What are you doing knocking so early?"

"I was hoping to talk to Jane."

"She's not here."

Because why would she be after I got the nerve to tell her how I feel? Just my luck.

Abigail storms up the stairs, holding a piece of paper. "Donny, did you know Jane was leaving?"

My spine tenses tighter than my guitar string. "No, I was just looking for her."

"What did you need?"

Heat shoots up my neck, and I'm convinced I resemble a clown with painted red cheeks. "I, uh, well, I uh just needed to talk to her."

Abigail pins me with her gaze. "Is that so?"

A phone ringing from inside her room probably just saved me from an interrogation. I turn to leave, but Shawna's words stop me. "Were you going to tell Jane you love her?"

Swiveling around, I lean my back against the wall. "What makes you ask me that?"

"I don't know. Maybe I just have a feeling," she says, heading down the stairs. "Let's get breakfast, okay?"

Some may think people with autism are not as smart as others, but I'm convinced they couldn't be farther from the truth. Shawna is observant and more intelligent than many people I've encountered over the years.

"How about you let me talk to Jane first, then I'll tell you what I say to her?"

Her lips turn into a full grin as I follow her into the kitchen. "It's a deal."

Shortly thereafter, Abigail joins us. "That was Clara."

"Does she know where Jane went?" I ask as a knot forms in my stomach.

Abigail pours a cup of coffee before giving a clipped, "Jane is heading to Pocahontas to see Tammy Sharp."

"My cousin? Why?" I ask, grabbing a box of Life cereal from the cabinet.

"Ever since Tammy saved her mama's life, Jane has been a little bit obsessed with her." Abigail blows on her coffee before taking a sip.

"Oh. I bet Clara told her to go."

"So, Donny, how would you feel about making the drive to Pocahontas? Jane's not answering her phone."

"Sure, I can do that," I answer Abigail like she's asking me a simple thing, but inside I'm jumping up and down like a teenage girl at a Jonas Brothers concert.

"I bet you can," Abigail says as she takes her coffee and heads up the stairs, laughter echoing in her footsteps.

Within the hour, I'm driving out of DeValls Bluff. My stomach clenches when a red Mustang convertible falls in behind me. The driver is wearing a ball cap, and I can't tell whether they're male or female. Wait a minute, there's no way that girl Genny could know I'm here. And if she did, I don't think she'd be stupid enough to come this far.

Satisfied that I'm being paranoid, I press the gas, excited to see Jane again.

Chapter 23

My heart skips a beat when Tammy Sharp opens the door to her super adorable ranch-style home. This woman is fire. She literally took out a serial killer here a while back. Let's get something straight. I am not advocating violence. But if someone kidnapped my mom, yeah, I'd do whatever it took to get her back. Her or my dad.

I have a dad.

A real live man, not just a figment of my imagination.

My mind is all over the place as Tammy wraps me in a hug. "Come on in."

Ruby Sharp, Tammy's mom, struts into the living area carrying a tray. Her pink joggers and matching sweatshirt, along with her blonde waves that fall to her shoulders, make me smile. "I made ham and cheese sliders and some chamomile tea," she says, glancing at Tammy. "Honey, you're out of ham."

"Okay, Mama, I'll add it to my pickup order. Jane, I have the guest bedroom ready for you."

"Thank you both. I can't tell you how much I appreciate you letting me stay the night here."

Ruby pops a plain potato chip in her mouth as she takes stock of me. "You must be starving. You look like you haven't eaten in days."

If you're from the South or have ever visited the South, you know most Southern women fifty or older don't have a filter, and Ruby Sharp is no exception. Still, I can't stop the grin from dancing across my lips as I scoop a slider off the tray. "I actually am starving."

My shoulders tense as I lock eyes with a brindle pit bull who prances right up to me. I eye him as he sits beside my leg.

Tammy clicks her tongue. "Leave our guest alone, Castle."

The dog, Castle, sniffs my shoe before crawling onto the couch beside Tammy and laying his head in her lap. She rubs behind his ear, and he falls asleep within seconds.

We continue eating, a comfortable silence echoing around the room. Ruby stands. "I'm taking my granddaughter, Alvie, to Lake Charles State Park tomorrow. Jane, we'd love for you to come with us."

I lean back into the soft cushions. "I've never been to that one, so I can get another stamp in my state park passport book."

"Oh, goodie." Ruby sets her drink on the side table, clapping her hands together. "There are two state parks within a few minutes of each other we like to visit. We'll have a picnic at Lake Charles, then tour the museum and courthouse at Powhatan. I think you'll love it."

"Thank you for the invite," I respond, appreciating the gesture.

"Oh, we might also invite Leo, my other granddaughter," she replies, a hint of excitement in her voice.

The situation surprises me. I didn't even know Tammy had any children. Would it be too nosy to ask how Ruby ended up with two granddaughters? Curiosity nudges me to take the plunge, so I leaned a little closer. "I didn't realize you had kids, Tammy."

Tammy smiles, her eyes lighting up. "Well, Alvie came to us last year. And Leo is actually Jace's daughter from his first marriage."

"Oh, okay. I'm sorry for being nosy," I apologize, feeling sheepish for prying into her personal life.

"It's no problem."

"How's Leo doing after the incident?" Ruby asks, lowering her voice and looking around like she's afraid of getting caught asking the question.

The front door clicks shut, revealing a dark-haired woman. "I'm doing okay. Just need to find a job."

I assume this is Leo. Her thick black hair bounces around her shoulders as she stops in the middle of the room. With her black leather pants and creamy skin, she reminds me of someone who would play the lead character in an action film.

Ruby stands, wrapping Leo in a hug. "Honey, I just worry about you."

"I know."

Tammy interrupts. "Leo, this is Jane Bennett. Jane, this is Leo Eubanks."

She turns a brilliant smile to me. "Hi, Jane. It's nice to meet you. In case you haven't been told, I just got fired from my job."

"I'm sorry to hear that."

Ruby settles back into her seat. "We all were."

"Listen, I was not in the best state of mind when my ex and I had it out," she says, her voice tinged with regret.

"That's understandable. Did he cheat on you?"

"I wish it were something like that. No, he went to prison for things I'd better not talk about right now," she replies, her eyes welling up with unshed tears. "All I can say is he is the worst man on the planet."

"Oh my, I'm so sorry. That's unimaginable," I whisper, my heart going out to Leo and her situation.

"Thanks. It's been a tough road. Hey, I've been watching your show, and I'm really sorry to hear you got the shaft like that," she adds, shifting the focus back to me.

I tug on my earlobe, shaking my head slightly as my situation takes on a new perspective. Instead of seeing what happened as a negative, maybe I need to change my outlook.

I'll spend the night, go to the state parks tomorrow, and then head back home to face my new situation.

Chapter 24

After today, I'm convinced the best way to take my mind off my troubles is to go to a state park or two. Arkansas isn't called the Natural State for no reason. By the time four thirty arrives, Ruby pulls into the driveway at Tammy's house.

Sunlight pours in through the front door as I follow Ruby inside, Leo and Alvie tagging behind. After cleaning up, we settle down in the living room.

Ruby turns on the television. "I hate to miss the

evening news."

A meteorologist in a pink dress discusses how the weather will hit eighty by the weekend. Good, I like warmer weather. I tune her out as my mind drifts to Theodore. It's time for me to face the music.

My brows furrow when the scene switches to a reporter standing in front of the houseboats from the design competition. What are they doing in DeValls Bluff?

The camera pans in on Theodore, who is standing beside the reporter.

Oh no, my stomach rolls as I clench the couch cushion.

"I'm Kaitlin Brady with KAIT news here with Theodore Baldwin for an update on the breaking story we first shared yesterday. Local designer Jane Bennett was a top contender to win Small Town, Big Design when she learned that the new guest judge is her biological father." She turns her gaze to Theodore. "What was it like finding out you have a long-lost daughter?"

Theodore rubs the back of his neck and blows a breath out. "At first, I was shocked. I mean, it was so unexpected, but now I couldn't be more thrilled."

"How did you feel when you discovered that your role as a judge inadvertently caused Jane to lose her top spot in the competition? That must have put quite a strain on your relationship."

"Yes, I can only imagine how shocking it was for Jane, just as it was for me. I know she's feeling hurt and confused right now."

"Do you know where she is at the moment?"

"She's taking some much-needed time away to think everything through and process her emotions." His words come out confident, as if he and I talked about the situation before I left.

"I can understand that. What are your next steps in light of all this?"

"My next steps, Kaitlin, will be to step down from my position as a judge so that Jane can compete in the finals without a conflict of interest."

She cocks her head. "Wait, you're really going to step down?"

"Absolutely. Jane has poured her heart and soul into this competition. I know it wasn't an easy journey, especially considering the many talented designers she faced off against to secure her place on the design show. Making it to the finale is a remarkable achievement. One she has truly earned. In contrast, I feel I don't deserve to be here, especially seeing the toll this has taken on my daughter."

"I know Jane is your daughter, but you just met. Why would you put your career on hold for someone you don't even know?"

"My heart knows her and loves her, so to me, this is hardly a sacrifice. I just hope she'll return to the show."

I sit straight up in the chair, my eyes welling with tears. What if there's a chance to build a relationship with my father? A real chance? How many years did I pray for this exact thing to happen? Not the design competition thing, but to meet my father. This is the answer to those prayers. Because what if I wasn't ready before now? Could it be that God had this moment in mind for Theodore and me?

Tammy sticks her head inside the house. "Donny just pulled in behind me. Jace is talking to him now."

Donny is here? My breath catches in my throat. Donny is here. Outside. Right now. Without thinking, I race out the door and straight into his arms.

Chapter 25

After bracing myself for Jane to be mad, I was not expecting her to fall into my arms. I am not complaining.

She presses her soft, warm lips to my cheek. "I'm so glad to see you!" she continues talking, but my vision has gone blurry, and I have no idea what she's saying.

Jane Gorgeous Bennett just kissed me. I've heard people say they get butterflies when they see a certain person or hear them talk, but I've never quite understood what they meant by "butterflies." Until this moment. I now know what it feels like to have a million of them in my stomach.

I'm going to kiss her for real. My lips are almost on hers.

Jane sucks in a deep breath. "I like mint gum," she blurts.

I surprise myself by laughing at her obvious attempt to keep me from kissing her.

Her eyes crinkle before she lays her head on my shoulder. I'd be content to stand here all day with her in my arms. Instead, I lay my chin on top of her head. "That was an amazing first kiss."

Her spine freezes, and she shoves away from me. "That was not our first kiss."

"Oh, really? When do you suggest we have our first kiss?" I lean in, trying to gauge her reaction, a playful grin spreading across my face. "I'm totally up for it right now, especially knowing how much you enjoy mint gum."

She rolls her eyes, but a tinge of pink creeps onto her cheeks as she glances away, flustered. "You're impossible," she replies, shaking her head. With a playful flick of her hair, she turns to walk toward the entrance, leaving me to catch up.

I chuckle as I follow her inside, the familiar scent of chocolate filling the air. "So, later then?"

Her pace slows for a moment as she turns back and smiles, a mischievous glint in her eyes. "Be careful, or I'll ask Tammy or Leo to take care of you," she teases, a hint of a giggle escaping her lips.

"What do you mean by that?" I ask, genuinely intrigued, as I furrow my brow, trying to picture Tammy as my potential protector in this ongoing game we're playing.

My great aunt, Ruby, pulls a pan from the oven. "I made a pan of brownies. Anyone interested?"

"Of course we are," Tammy says.

Ruby waves a spatula in the air. "By the way, dear, you need to pick up more cocoa. I used the last."

Jace Eubanks, Tammy's husband, barks out a sudden laugh. "I'm so happy you live next door, or I may never get such delicious-smelling treats."

Tammy swipes Jace with a towel she pulled from the stove. "You hush your mouth. I can bake."

Ruby takes off her apron and heads to the front door. "Y'all enjoy the brownies. I have something to do real quick." She stops at the door and yells down the hall. "Leo, I need your help."

Within five minutes, Ruby returns, catches my eye, and winks. I try to speak, but she shakes her finger at me. I wonder about her odd behavior, but since she's a Sharp and we've been called weird before, I ignore it. No one would know we only started spending more time together after Jane read an article about Tammy saving Ruby from a sociopath. Our busy lives had pushed family time aside, but we all agreed to do better and spend more time together.

Many laughs and several hugs later, Jane and I walk outside. "I'm so glad you get to stay in the competition."

"Me too. I'll see you back at the cabin?"

"Yep, I'll follow you."

I open the driver's door of Jane's Jeep and step back.

Jane eyes me before stepping inside. She sticks the key in the ignition and frowns.

"What is it?" I glance at Jane with concern.

"My Jeep won't start."

"That's strange. Have you been having trouble with it starting lately?"

"Not at all," Jane says, crossing her arms as she stares at the dashboard, which remains silent.

"Pop the hood. I'll see if I can figure out what it is."

Ruby bounces down the steps. "There's no time for that. Jane, you should ride with Donny. I'll have Jace look at your Jeep, and we'll bring it to you."

"Really?" Jane's eyebrows shoot up.

"Yes, we'll be happy to."

"I need to get back to the competition to speak to Theodore and the producer." Jane pauses. "I hate to put you out, though. That's a long drive."

"It's no trouble. We'll take care of things here and see you soon," Ruby says, turning to me with a wink like we're coconspirators in a heist.

As Jane and I drive away, I can't help but wonder if Ruby didn't do this on purpose when she left the house earlier. And if so, I owe her one.

Chapter 26

That was definitely not a kiss. Over the years, I've pecked a bunch of guys on the cheek, maybe even a dozen that I had no romantic interest in whatsoever. I ball my hand into a fist, extending a finger as I try to tally them up in my mind.

Growing up with Clara, I'm pretty sure I gave her dad a kiss on the cheek at least once.

Then there's Robert DeWitt, who comes to mind. After he encouraged me when I forgot my lines in a school play in third grade, I kissed his cheek. I tap my chin and close my eyes for a sec.

I can picture myself kissing Mr. Hillard on the cheek after a Sunday service one morning when I was ten. He's an older gentleman I've known forever, with kind eyes and a wealth of stories to share. He offered to teach me how to drive. He stepped up many times over the years. Now I realize it was because I didn't have a dad to help.

I really need to thank them both.

There's a total of three fingers. See, I have kissed men on the cheek before. With an inward groan, I realize all those times were when I was a kid. I'm no longer a kid.

My eyes shift to Donny. His muscles bulge as he turns the wheel. When did he get those?

What am I thinking? Come on, Jane, get a grip.

My gaze drifts out the window, watching as the houses dissolve into sprawling fields, the scenery shifting as we drive toward the interstate, leaving Pocahontas behind.

"What are you over there counting?" Donny interrupts my self-degrading.

With a flash of a smile, I determine to put the

not-kiss behind me. No sense in focusing on something that meant nothing. My stomach pitches, but I ignore it. "Nothing important. Just thinking."

"About Theodore Baldwin?" His voice is soft, understanding.

"No, not him," I reply instantly regretting it.

"Oh? I'd love to know what's running through your mind."

Donny is right. A spark of frustration ignites within me. There's absolutely no reason for my mind to dwell on that insignificant kiss on the cheek, especially with a far more urgent matter that needs to be addressed. Theodore and the competition.

Waves of heat rushes to my chest, and I breathe through my nose and out my mouth to steady myself. "If you want to know the truth," I say, glancing at Donny, who keeps his eyes on the road, "I was actually counting how many men I've kissed on the cheek over the years. And let me tell you, the number is definitely more than one."

A bark of laughter erupts from the truck cab, the sound rich against the engine's rumble beneath us. "You're putting an awful lot of thought into a kiss you claimed wasn't even an actual kiss," he teases, a playful gleam in his eyes as he steals a sideways glance at me.

"I am not," I retort, my voice slightly defensive, though I can't help but feel a hint of amusement.

"Okay then, how many?" he presses, a wicked grin spreading across his face.

"How many what?" I respond with feigned innocence.

"How many men have you kissed? On the cheek, of course," he clarifies, his grin widening as the teasing tone persists.

"I'm not telling you any confidential information." I tease back.

"Fair enough." He glances in the rearview mirror, then checks the side mirrors to ensure the road is clear. With a steady grip on the wheel, he shifts into the passing lane, maneuvering around a massive truck carrying a load of logs.

I glance at my phone when Clara's name flashes across the screen.

Hey.

Hey

CLARA

Archer got hit with a football.

JANE

Is he okay?

CLARA

Yeah, his back hurts so I need to stay here until he's up.

JANE

No problem!

CLARA

Is Donny with you?

JANE

Yes, how do you know?

CLARA

You're both at the same location.

JANE

I forgot you're like the FBI with tracking people

CLARA

Haha

> Tell Archer I hope he feels better soon.

Will do. Love you. And you're gonna be okay.

> I know. Love you too.

After explaining the texts to Donny, we settle into a companionable silence for a while. A few minutes more into the drive, a deep growl escapes from my stomach, so I lay my flat palm over it, hoping to muffle the sound.

Donny cuts his eyes my way, a sweet smile dominating his face. "Do you want to stop for a bite to eat?"

"Sure," I reply, my face heating up. I pull up the navigation on my phone, searching for nearby restaurants. "Looks like we can have gas station chicken or gas station chicken."

"Well, then, lead the way to Chester's Chicken."

Even though my mind is mostly on food, I can't help but think about what it would be like to go on an actual date with Donny Sharp.

My mouth waters as I stare at the display full of food. Last time I ate at a gas station, I got a burrito, and it was so cheesy good. But that crispy fried chicken looks like it just came out of the grease.

I glance at Donny, tapping his foot in front of the cooler. He pulls out two cherry Dr. Peppers before walking back to where I am. My heart flops.

"What can I get you, hon?" The gray-haired lady behind the counter smiles, her eyes crinkling with kindness as she wipes her hands on a flour-dusted apron.

"Um, I can't decide between the chicken or the burrito," I say, glancing at the menu hanging above us. "Donny, you go ahead and order while I'm thinking," I add.

Donny glances at me, a playful sparkle lighting up his blue eyes. "Come on, Jane, get both. You know you want to."

His enthusiasm is infectious, and I can't help but smile. "That's a lot of food, though," I reply, eyeing the chicken.

He nudges me with his shoulder. "How about we both get the chicken, some tater babies, and rolls? Then we can share a burrito for fun," he suggests.

The aroma of fried chicken and spices wafts through the air, making my stomach growl in agreement. "That sounds good."

With our hands full, we load into Donny's truck. He hands me a cherry Dr. Pepper. "Is this still your favorite drink?"

"It is. I can't believe you remember that," I say, taking the drink from him.

He places a hand over mine. "There's not much about you I could ever forget."

My eyes widen as I twist the cap off the cherry Dr. Pepper.

Donny clamps his gaze onto mine like he's searching for something. What? I don't know. What I do know is that we are both holding our breath. It takes some effort, but I untangle our eyes and take a swig of my cherry Dr. Pepper.

"Will you bless the food?" I ask the first thing that pops into my mind.

After the blessing, Donny snatches the burrito out of the bag and holds it up. "Want the first bite?"

I shift my weight from one side to the other, trying to get comfortable and keep my stomach from being queasy. "You go ahead." I bite a chunk of the roll off. "I really just want this roll right now."

Donny smirks before sinking his teeth into the burrito. Chili and cheese squirt out, landing on his finger. He licks it off, the stupid smirk still on his face, before holding the burrito close to my mouth. "Your turn."

My breath leaves me. "Oh, you can just cut it into."

"What's wrong? Scared of getting cooties or something?"

"Not at all. I uh I uh just..." Words escape me, so I pull out the chicken leg and tear a piece off.

Donny has the nerve to chuckle. I glare at him before popping the chicken into my mouth. I turn my head toward the window before he can take another bite of the burrito.

"What's been the best part of your time on the design show so far?" he asks, sipping his cherry Dr. Pepper.

A big smile spreads across my face. "Honestly, the entire experience has been amazing, or it was before I got kicked off. But meeting Martha Meadows? That's definitely my highlight. I've been a fan of hers since I was a kid, watching her flip houses on TV."

"I remember you and Clara watching her show," Donny says with a smile as he puts his leftovers in the bag. He hands me my half of the burrito before merging onto the highway.

Why am I making a big deal out of the burrito? I've eaten after Donny before. It's no biggie. To prove it, I sink my teeth into the cheesy goodness. And I know I'll never look at burritos the same.

Chapter 27

As soon as we pull into the driveway at the cabin, Abigail streaks out the front door and jerks Jane's door open. "Are you okay? Why haven't you been answering your phone?"

"Honestly, I just needed some space. I'm sorry for being childish," Jane says, stepping out of the truck.

Abigail pulls Jane into a hug. "I'm just glad you're okay. Clara told me about your Jeep," Abigail says, with a wink at me. "It's a good thing Donny was there to bring you back."

Wait a minute. Was everyone in on the Jeep not starting? If so, I owe a lot of people a big thank you.

Jane steps away from Abigail, grabs her blue jean purse out of the back seat, and heads toward the cabin, arm in arm with Abigail. "I agree."

"Sweetheart, are you up for having a late dinner with Theo?"

"After what he said on KAIT, I'd come off as a total jerk to say no. As long as it's a family meal, I'm all in."

"Absolutely. Theo offered to bring Craig's Barbecue here. How does that sound?"

"Sounds amazing. Oh, Donny, that includes you," she adds with a playful smile, casting a glance in my direction.

A soothing warmth envelops my chest at her words. Does that mean she sees me as part of her family? As long as it's not that awkward brotherly vibe, I'm all on board.

"Of course it includes Donny."

"I'm looking forward to it," I say as silence greets us when we enter the cabin. "I'm surprised Shawna isn't already out here."

"Oh, her daddy came and got her this morning."

"That stinks," Jane and I say at the same time.

We laugh and meet each other's gaze.

Abigail looks at us for a moment before walking into the kitchen. "I'll make some tea."

Jane breaks our locked gazes first. She tugs a chunk of blonde hair behind her ear. "Sounds good. I'm gonna take a shower."

With a shout, I dart past her. "I'd better get mine before you use all the hot water."

A hand darts out from behind me, shoving me into the wall. "Oh no, you don't, mister."

"Alright then, Chuck." I entwine my fingers with hers, fully expecting her to pull away.

Instead, she looks up at me and whispers, "Why are you here?"

Somehow, I manage to speak. "Because I brought you from Pocahontas."

She slips her fingers from mine but stays close. "No, why did you come to DeValls Bluff?"

My spine tenses at the question. I hesitate, unsure of how to articulate my situation without sounding melodramatic or paranoid. It feels strange to admit that I have a stalker. "Hiding from an obsessed teenager," I say, my voice low.

"What do you mean?" Jane asks, her expression shifting from curiosity to concern.

"There's this girl. She's been to at least ten of our concerts over the past year. She's convinced we're destined to be together. She always buys backstage passes, too. It was cute at first, you know? Just another teen with a crush." I run a hand through my hair, trying to gather my thoughts. "But then it got weird. Her mom used to bring her along, but after she turned eighteen, she started showing up on her own."

"Maybe she's just a hardcore fan," Jane suggests lightly, but there's unease in her tone.

I take a deep breath, tightening my grip on my belt loop. "It escalated. One night, she showed up at my apartment."

"Oh," she replies, her eyes wide with shock. "That's... really serious."

"I thought about this place and figured I'd spend some time fishing with Jesse and finding a peaceful hideaway. I promise I had no idea you were here," I say, my gaze dropping to Jane's lips.

"Thanks for being honest," she replies, her voice warm.

"You mean a lot to me, and you deserve the truth, no

filters, just the truth." The words catch in my throat, and my thoughts jumble.

With a graceful movement and doe-eyed brown gaze, Jane leans in, pressing her soft lips to mine.

And the world as I know it changes from the U2 song "I Still Haven't Found What I'm Looking For" to "The Power of Love" by Huey Lewis and the News.

Chapter 28

My brain fizzles. My heart soars, and I think I may fall into the wall beside Donny if I don't stop this kiss. I lean back and whisper, "Now *that* was our first kiss."

Donny's lips curve into a smile. "Yes, it was."

"I hope you enjoyed it because it's also our last."

"I disagree."

"I'm serious, Donny. There's too much going on in my life to complicate things further with a relationship."

"That's not fair," he says, slapping the wall.

Donny's open handed slap against the hard sheetrock echoes down the hall. My gaze widens, but I stay firm. "Fair or not, it's the way it has to be. What if I end up moving due to my career? I've worked so hard for this moment, and I can't give it up." I press a kiss to his cheek before walking away.

I slink into my room and lock the door before falling face-first onto the bed. With a moan, I smash my pillow onto my face and squeal. I don't know what possessed me to kiss Donny, and I don't care. It happened. I'm glad it did, as my last words to him play over in my mind. He needs to understand that I can't focus on anything but my career right now. Theodore is enough of a distraction as it is.

Rain pelts against the window frame as I tap Face-Time on my phone.

Within seconds, Clara answers. "Why are you hiding behind a pillow?"

"Because," I say, my voice muffled.

"What did you do?" There's a smugness in her tone that makes me think Donny has already told her. But he hasn't had time.

I move the pillow half a millimeter, just enough so part of one eye sticks out. "Something spur of the moment that I may or may not regret."

Clara pins her arms across her chest. "Spill."

I intertwine my hands and take a deep breath, eyeballing the rain on the river through my open curtains. "I kissed Donny."

She freezes, eyes wide, and she turns away from the phone. "Archer! You were right! Jane kissed Donny!"

"I told you it would happen," Archer says from somewhere inside the room.

I stick my hands underneath my legs. "Clara Dean! It was just a peck. Don't make it a big deal."

"Yeah, yeah. Just a peck? Where did the peck take place?"

"In the hallway."

"Did you peck his cheek again, or did you upgrade to his lips this time?"

Someone pounds on the door. "Everyone can hear you talking to Clara about how you kissed my lips," Donny yells through the door.

Clara and Archer both break into hysterical laughter.

"Hey, Clara," Donny continues, "Jane said it won't

happen again. Will you talk some sense into her?"

I pinch the bridge of my nose. Could this get any more public? "I need to get ready for dinner with Theodore," I say, an edge to my voice.

That's all it takes to sober Clara up. "I wish I were there so I could support you, Jane. But I know all will work out. Archer and I have been praying for the best outcome for you. We love you so much."

"I love you both as well."

"Let me know how it goes tonight."

"Will do."

"Jane, Theo is here," Mom says from outside my door.

"Okay, I'll be out in a minute." I throw my hair in a bun and slip on my fuzzy pink slippers before heading to see Theodore.

Theodore leans his elbow on the kitchen island across from where Mom stands, stirring a glass of sweet tea. He says something I can't make out. Mom laughs, her tone melodic. She looks happy. Ever since she and Archer's dad, John Banks, broke up last month, so he could move to Italy to run the company where he serves as CEO, she's been down. But not today.

I clear my throat as I enter the room. Plates of barbecue, chips, buns, bowls of sauces, and slaw line the island. A sweet yet citrusy aroma snags my senses, and my mouth literally waters.

Theodore's face lights up with a warm, infectious smile as he looks at me. "Jane. I'm truly delighted you came back."

I lift a shoulder, trying to downplay the flutter of emotions in my chest. "I kinda had to after catching your news segment on KAIT."

His eyes shimmer with sincerity. "I meant every word I said."

I raise an eyebrow, skeptical. "You don't even know me."

With an earnest expression, he replies, "That's true, but I promise you, I genuinely want to know you better. Would you be open to the possibility of getting to know one another?"

I pause, considering his hopeful demeanor, and nod. "I suppose that would be okay. I'm always down for another country breakfast."

He grins. "Absolutely. I met with Martha Meadows after the segment. She was not happy I did that without getting her involved, but she and the network are discussing their options."

A sliver of hope settles in my chest. "So they may let me come back?"

"I can't promise anything, but they are at least considering it."

Donny strolls into the kitchen, droplets of water cascading down his face from his damp hair, glistening as they land on his shoulders. My gaze falls to the slit in his T-shirt, which leaves just enough space for his leather necklace featuring a red guitar pick.

My heartbeat matches the rumble of thunder vibrating over the river. What were Theodore and I talking about? Right now, all I know is Donny wore the same shirt onstage last year when Clara and I went to one of his concerts. I can still feel the rock energy radiating from him. He didn't really affect me then. Or at least I didn't let him. But now? Now I narrow my eyes and promise myself that one day, that shirt will be mine.

Chapter 29

Back at the competition, Walter Jenkins, the host, leans forward, propping his bony elbows on the fold-up table, a spark of excitement dancing in his puppy dog eyes. "Jane, Jane, Jane. I am simply thrilled! Ever since your little..." he pauses, waving his hand with exaggerated flair, "...incident, our ratings have soared to an astonishing three times what they were before."

I force a smile, wishing he would get to the point.

"That's good at least."

Lisa Flowers crosses her arms over her chest. "Good? It's fantastic. Not to mention, there's a buzz surrounding the new show that surpasses our wildest expectations. The network can't deny that it makes sense to bring you back."

"Great!"

"Are you willing to do what it takes to keep this momentum going?" Lisa cocks her head as she meets my gaze.

"Um, what exactly do you mean by what it takes?"

"After the sponsors weighed in, the executives had another emergency meeting. They agreed, but there's a condition to your returning to the show." Walter grins at me like he's just given me the best news ever.

"What kind of condition?" My spine tenses as I brace myself for what he has to say.

"Martha Meadows mentioned keeping Theodore on set as a mentor for you, and they're bringing in Shania Poppins for Jackson Welch," Lisa says.

I shrug. The condition could've been a lot worse. "I'm fine with that."

Walter slaps the desk. "We want to see some emotional conversations. People will eat that up, I promise."

"Look, I'm here to win a competition, not air my dirty laundry." I'm supposed to be in a design competition, not a reality show.

"I understand, really I do." Lisa walks around the desk and sits in the chair directly beside mine.

Swiveling my body, I anchor my gaze to Lisa's. "Then you need to understand that my relationship with Theodore Baldwin is personal, but I'm happy to discuss my design process or anything related to the show."

She shakes her head as her lips dance around a smile. "Jane, you've already got people's attention by the way you embrace the eighties. Honestly, you are adorable. Why not keep people interested by showing a little vulnerability with Theo?"

"I mean, I'm sure we'll talk, but I won't allow the network to focus on my life. Jackson deserves just as much screen time as I do."

"Yes, we agree. Then it's settled," Walter says.

"By the way, how do you feel about doing a magazine interview? Designing With Purpose wants you on their next cover."

I smile even though my brain just turned to mush.

One of the best design magazines wants me on its cover? I pinch myself. Nope, not dreaming.

The Prairie County Museum has so many artifacts. I don't know where to look first. My mind is focused on gathering as much information as possible about the hotel. The more I know, the better I'll be at designing the area I'm assigned.

Miss Lena, the director, a stunning woman with kind eyes, points at a mannequin wearing a beautiful antique wedding dress. "This is our bride with no name. We received a chest with the dress, but we don't know who it belonged to yet."

My fingers itch to run down the dress, but I keep my hands to myself. "Wow, that's amazing."

An hour later, I leave the museum with pictures of the displays and a lot more information than when I arrived. One interesting thing I found out is that the original hotel burned down, and the current building is a hundred years old.

The Castleberry Hotel stands as a captivating time capsule, brimming with forgotten moments and hidden stories. As we step into what was once the grand foyer, a delightful thrill wells up inside me. Above me, the intricate tin ceilings unfold like a shimmering tapestry, heightening my anticipation for this project. I can almost envision the skilled craftsmen of yester-year, meticulously installing each ornate piece with care and precision, their dedication echoing through time.

I glimpse the cameraman aiming the lens in my direction, prompting me to flash my most radiant design-show smile. They need to announce my area so I can start working here. If I had the money, I'd buy the hotel and renovate every room.

Theodore walks inside, stopping when he reaches me. "Hi, Jane."

My spine tenses. Could he be cozying up to me as my father so his show does well? Is that it? "Hello." I grit out.

The cameraman gets closer. I fix my face and point across the room. "Look how gorgeous this room is. I picture a beautiful staircase right there."

"The mayor wanted me to ask you about Donny. Would you see if his band would be interested in playing at the festival? The lead singer of the band they had booked has the flu."

"I can do that."

Jackson takes his place next to me, prompting Theo to retreat to stand by Mom. Jackson looks me up and down. I can only imagine what he thinks of the light purple tie-dyed jeans, black shirt, and black boots. "Nice shoes."

"Thanks."

As the production assistant informs us we're moments away from beginning, a wave of calm washes over me, loosening and uncoiling my spine.

The host clears his throat. "Hello, and welcome to Small Town, Big Design! I'm your host, Walter Jenkins. Today, we'll announce which areas our contestants will redo at the historic Castleberry Hotel. I have a number in my hand," he says, holding up a card, "and the contestant closest to this number will get first choice of the area they will redesign."

"Before we start, I want to remind everyone to come out next Friday and Saturday for the festival right here in downtown DeValls Bluff. I promise you don't want to miss it! Good luck to you both. Jackson, you were selected at random to pick the first number between one and one hundred. What is your number?"

"Fifty-seven."

"Alright, Jane, what is your number?"

"Seventy-three."

The host flips the card. "Jackson Welch is the closest contestant to number forty-five. You can now select either the foyer or the sitting area."

"Definitely the sitting area, Walter."

"That means, Jane, you have the foyer." He checked his watch. "You each have five weeks to make your space the top design. May the best designer win!"

Several hours later, the design is laid out, and I have ordered the supplies needed to bring my vision to life. As I spin around the room, Mom texts that she's outside to pick me up. I grab my bag and head for the exit, waving at the cameraman stationed near the door.

What I wouldn't do to have Donny or Shawna here helping me. And my Jeep. Donny had to leave this morning to meet with his agent, and Aunt Olivia is on her way here with Shawna. As far as the Jeep goes, I haven't even taken the time to reach out to Ruby. I'll do that when I get home.

As we pull into the drive, I see three cars, and I squeal when I notice one of them is my Jeep.

Donny and Leo both wave when I step out of

Mom's Highlander. They look awfully cozy leaning against Donny's Ford. Leo is Tammy's stepdaughter, so that means Donny and she are not related. Not blood anyway.

'I swallow the acid creeping up my throat as I stop beside them. Donny stands straight and meets my gaze. "Are you okay?"

"Yes, of course. Why?"

"You look mad."

"Well, I'm not," I snap. "Thank you for bringing my Jeep home, Leo. I forgot to reach out to Ruby."

Mom pats my shoulder and gives me the side-eye.

Leo waves a hand in the air. "You're welcome. Donny and I have been texting back and forth, so it's no problem."

A burning sensation crawls up my stomach and jabs me in my chest. I narrow my eyes at Donny. "Hey, the band they booked for the festival is out of commission. Would your band be interested? I don't need your help at the hotel."

"Yeah, I asked my agent to clear our schedule after one last show so I could focus on helping you at the hotel." Donny's facial muscles visibly twitch. "But give the mayor my number, and I'll work it out."

"Will do." Instead of asking if Donny and Leo would like some privacy, I hold my tongue. I mean, what if they say yes? "Did y'all want to come inside?"

Ruby pokes her head out the front door. "I'm already here! Had to use the bathroom. Leo, let's visit for a while before we head back."

I stomp up the steps, each footfall reverberating in my chest, drowning out my swirling thoughts. The heat coursing through me is like fire, igniting an urge to scream in frustration. For years, I've convinced myself I have no interest in Donny Sharp. But deep down, buried under layers of denial, I can no longer ignore the truth: I've been the biggest liar of all time.

Chapter 30

The drive from DeValls Bluff to Des Arc is leisurely, stretching for about fifteen minutes along a winding country road lined with tall, swaying trees and fields. As we cruise along, Jane rolls down her window, and a breeze carries the sweet scent of strawberry shortcake into the car. "Mm, that smells incredible," I remark, inhaling deeply.

Her head turns sharply in my direction, curiosity etched on her face. "What does?"

"Whatever strawberry stuff you're wearing," I reply, smiling.

"Oh! It's probably my lip gloss and shampoo," she says, a hint of a smile coloring her tone as she dabs her lips.

"I'm happy you decided to join me for dinner," I say, warmth filling my chest. "Even though you don't want to pursue what's happening between us."

"Well, we did owe each other a rain check, so there's that," she responds, a playful glint in her eyes. "I'm looking forward to getting to know Summer and Jesse a little better."

"Yeah, they were all for meeting us since they are already in Des Arc. I think you'll fall in love with Kristi's Kitchen. They have everything from fish to burgers. And all good," I assure her as we take a winding bend in the road.

A deer bursts from the edge of the woods, its graceful form momentarily frozen in the headlights. I ease off the accelerator, and the deer locks its big, innocent eyes on us for a fleeting moment. With a mighty leap, it bounds away into the safety of the trees on the other side of the road.

"That was a close one," Jane says. "I heard there were

deer all over the place, now I believe it."

"Definitely. I'm just glad we didn't hit her. I still can't believe you made me drive your pink Jeep." I widen my eyes, like I'm shocked and disgusted.

Jane sticks her tongue out at me. "You're the one who offered to drive."

"Yeah, my truck."

"Quit whining. You know you love driving my Jeep."

We make the rest of the trip in a comfortable silence, my mind racing with ideas on how to get Jane to change her mind about us dating.

Kristi's Kitchen is a hidden gem nestled in the heart of Des Arc, famous for its warm atmosphere and delectable locally caught fish. Dad used to have a few clients in the area who commissioned custom wood furniture from him. Sometimes he would let me and Clara tag along on his trips, and our favorite part was always the stop here for a plate of their crispy fried fish. Now, I get to share this special place with Jane, and I just know she'll love it as much as I do.

As I park on the side of the road, my leg bounces with excitement. The familiar wooden sign sways in the breeze, and I can already imagine the welcoming smell when we open the door.

Once we're seated, my fingers tap on the polished wooden table while we wait for Jesse and Summer to join us.

"While you were filming today," I say, breaking the silence, "the mayor stopped by and talked to me about the band playing at the festival."

Jane's eyes light up. "Did you agree?"

"I did," I confirm, a smile creeping onto my face.

"Okay, great! I figured you would, so I've been asking around for another helper," she replies, a hint of relief in her voice.

"I thought you didn't need my help." I narrow my gaze.

"That's the truth. You're too distracting."

I file that comment away to use later. "You should ask Leo," I suggest, my gaze drifting to a wall decorated with a large map along with photographs of people holding their freshly caught fish. I know that somewhere in that collage, my dad is grinning as he displays his own prized catch.

"Why?" Jane asks, blotches of red staining her cheeks. "Do you want her here for some reason?"

I can't believe Jane is acting like she's jealous. "No,

she's just bored staying with Tammy and Jace."

This is the best thing ever. Now, to decide whether I play this up or let Jane know there's no way in the world I'd date my cousin. Even if she is kin through marriage and not by blood.

Gross.

Jesse and Summer bustle around the corner. "Sorry, we're late. My sister tried to talk me into letting her come meet you," Summer says to Jane.

Jane looks up from the menu, a light smile flitting across her face. "I'd be happy to meet her anytime."

"Boy, I am starving," Jesse interjects. "I'm ordering the biggest fish plate they have on the menu."

"Same goes for me," Jane says.

I meet her green eyes and wink. For the first time, I can honestly say I'm thankful for the obsessed girl. If not for her, I may have waited until later in the summer to visit Jesse.

Yep, thank the Lord for teenage girls with a crush. Until they show up in person. I blink my eyes a few times as someone who looks just like Genny Weather-ston slides into a chair at the table next to ours.

Chapter 31

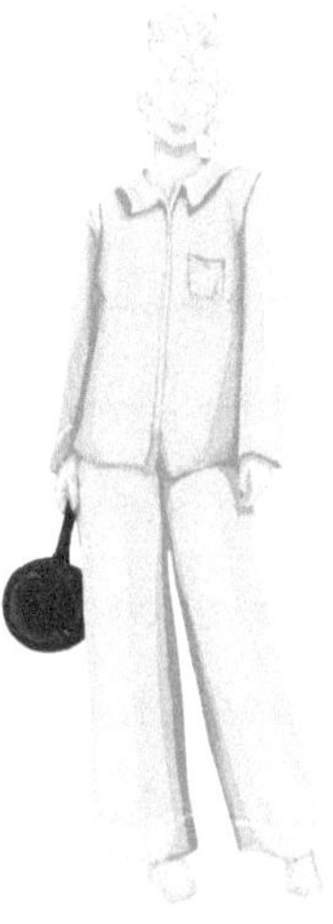

Donny bursts out of his chair so suddenly that I gasp, the sound escaping my lips before I can stop it. "What are you doing here?" His voice trembles slightly.

I follow his frantic gaze, and my stomach twists into knots at the sight. It's the same girls from the other day, and they've brought another friend.

Genny, the boldest of the bunch, tilts her head defiantly, her long, dark hair cascading over one shoulder.

"It's a free country. We can eat anywhere we like," she declares, a smirk playing on her lips.

"Not when your crush has turned into something creepy," Donny fires back, his voice sharp, and I can see the anger brewing beneath the surface.

The couple at the counter turns around to observe the scene.

Jesse, still clad in his police uniform, rises from his seat, the fabric of his shirt stretching taut against his broad shoulders. "Ladies, please join me outside," he says, his demeanor calm yet commanding.

The blonde girl's eyes widen in alarm, and she nearly tumbles out of her seat as she scrambles to her feet. "I'm not going to jail for you," she stammers, glancing nervously at her friends, who exchange an uneasy look.

"We're not going to jail," the girl with big, black-rimmed glasses asserts, though her voice wavers, betraying her uncertainty. "Are we?"

"That depends." Jesse turns his gaze back to Donny. "Want to fill me in on who they are?"

"This is the girl who stopped by my apartment uninvited," Donny replies, his voice firm but quieter now, as if the tension is draining away.

"Come outside now," Jesse insists, employing his firm, authoritative tone that brooks no argument.

"So, that's the girl who came to your apartment?" I ask, my gaze following them until the door shuts.

"Yep."

"I hate to tell you this, but I saw her at Craig's the other day. She was nice, but I got major creeper vibes."

"Maybe I should've pressed charges."

"I let them know how her obsession with you could cause problems if you decide to press charges. I don't think they'll be back," Jesse says as he reclaims his seat.

With the tension diffused, we settle into our fish plates, savoring the crispy fillets and the tangy tartar sauce.

Jesse glances at his watch. "I hate that we have to leave so early."

Summer opens her mouth but shuts it when Jesse shakes his head. "Oh yes, we do have to leave. Jane, try their ice cream."

A few minutes later, vanilla ice cream drips down my spoon, the sweet, creamy texture melting in my mouth as I shoot Donny a sideways glare and open the conversation we started before Summer and Jesse arrived. "I'll find someone to help with the design," I insist, trying to suppress a hint of irritation. "I don't want to ask Leo to come all this way for no reason."

Donny leans back against the wooden park bench, a teasing grin stretching across his face. "She'd get to be on national television. I bet she'll jump at the chance."

"It's really fine," I reply, my tone clipped.

"Do you dislike Leo for some reason?" he probes, his brow arching in playful suspicion.

"What? No, of course not." I shake my head, trying to sound convincing.

"Really? Because you're acting like you're jealous of my cousin," Donny continues, his voice dripping with mock seriousness.

"Y'all are not blood relatives," I retort, trying to brush it off.

"Gross, Jane. You need to get your mind out of the gutter. I don't care if there's no blood relation; you couldn't pay me to date Leo," he replies, wrinkling his nose in exaggerated disgust.

"She's gorgeous, though," I counter, unable to deny her beauty.

"Yuck! Can you imagine family dinners? All those kinfolk crammed around the table, sharing stories, and awkward silences. Hard pass for me," he says, shuddering theatrically.

I scoop another mouthful of the rich vanilla, contemplating his words. "Yeah, that would definitely be weird. I'd never date a cousin by marriage either, so I get where you're coming from," I agree, shaking my head with a chuckle.

"It's okay that you're jealous," Donny insists, a glint in his hazel eyes as he takes a leisurely bite of his chocolate fudge sundae.

The velvety soft ice cream sticks to my throat, and I spiral into a fit of coughs.

Donny stands and makes his way around the table, concern mingling with his teasing demeanor.

"Are you ready to head out?" I ask.

"No, I was actually going to give you mouth-to-mouth," he says.

Just then, his phone buzzes on the tabletop. He glances at the screen, and the lighthcarted atmosphere shifts as he sighs, the playful look replaced by a serious one. "It's my agent," he explains, his voice tinged with reluctance. "I need to take this."

"Go ahead," I say, my voice trembling as he steps away. The fleeting warmth of his smile lingers as I scoop the last remnants of my melted ice cream. The sweet, sugary taste mingles with my swirling thoughts. I need to tell Clara how I feel about her brother.

I wonder if a few days apart will help me sort through this confusing mix of emotions. Is this just a simple attraction, or is it something deeper? I push aside the persistent voice in my head that reminds me of the spark, the zing I feel whenever we touch.

Ever since watching Hotel Transylvania as a kid, I've dreamed of experiencing that euphoric zing moment, that perfect connection with someone. But it never came. Until Donny. The thought sends a rush of warmth through me, and I realize perhaps I need another scoop of ice cream. Or maybe five. I need something to soothe the turmoil churning within me.

Donny slides into the seat across from me, his lips tugged downwards. "My agent just called to remind me about a show tomorrow night. Like I could ever forget something that important."

"Oh? Where exactly is the show?" I inquire, curiosity piqued.

"Believe it or not, it's in Texarkana, of all places," he replies, rolling his eyes slightly but with a smile tugging at the corners of his mouth. "I need to hit the road tonight if I want to make it in time."

"How fun! When will you be back?" I ask, trying to mask the twinge of disappointment at the thought of him leaving.

He leans forward, his fingers entwining with mine, sending a rush of warmth through me. The soft brush of his thumb against mine is both comforting and intimate. "I should be back in a few days. We're going to get ready for the festival at our studio," he says, but I catch a glimmer of reluctance in his gaze.

I jerk my hand away and give him a dirty look. A part of me realizes that with Donny gone a while, I can see how I really feel. But a bigger part wants to ask if I can go. Especially with the way waves of tingles are moving from my hand to my heart.

Chapter 32

With Donny away on his band adventure, the cabin feels unusually quiet, almost too still. I wander into the kitchen, the scent of pine mingling with the fresh morning air from the open window, and grab a bright red apple from the fruit bowl for breakfast. As I take a bite, the juicy sweetness bursts in my mouth, momentarily lifting my spirits.

My phone buzzes on the countertop, pulling me out of my thoughts. I glance at the screen and see a flurry of notifications. Locals are abuzz on social media about Donny's band, Donny Sharp and the Nostalgic Echoes, performing at the music festival.

I open the sliding glass doors and settle on the island, staring at the view. A breeze wafts through, lifting my hair. I close my eyes and breathe in the fresh air.

Mom lumbers down the hallway, her suitcase on rolling wheels screeching against the wood floor. "Morning, Jane," she says, kissing my cheek.

"Morning, Mom. Hey, thank you for staying here the past few days."

"Not a problem. You and Donny needed a chaperone, and besides, I enjoyed the time away from my daily life. Ever since John and I broke up..." she pauses, staring outside.

"Are you sure you don't want me to have Tammy Sharp pay him a visit?" I ask, my tone teasing.

"Ha! I thought about it. But seriously, we both figured it was the right call since he'd be in Italy for a long while. He didn't break up with me," she says, flipping her hair like she owns the room.

"Oh, he'd be a fool to break up with my foxy mama," I tease, a broad grin spreading across my face as I fondly remind Mom of the nickname I gave her when I was little. "I mean, come on, you're definitely still foxy," I add, trying to catch her eye.

Mom chuckles. "I'm foxy, huh? Well, I'll take that as a compliment."

As the laughter settles, she turns serious. "But all jokes aside, our breakup was for the best. Our lifestyles are just too different, especially now that he's back as CEO of the company. The pressure is just... different."

I take a sip of my coffee, then set the mug down, leaning forward. "I've noticed how you've been looking at Theodore Baldwin lately."

She raises an eyebrow, crossing her arms. "Theodore Baldwin? That sounds so formal."

I shrug. "What can I say? I've only known him by that title."

Her expression softens for a moment. "Well, he's your father, after all."

"I know," I reply, my tone shifting. "And maybe one day we'll have a closer relationship. Right now, though, I'm not so sure how I feel about it."

"Why's that?" she asks, concern creeping into her voice.

"Because I can't shake the feeling he's using the media to boost his own career, and I'm just a pawn in his game." I lean back, remembering the moment I saw him on TV. "I mean, he practically declared his love for me on live television, then claimed he stepped down from his judgeship to be a more accessible father figure. It just felt... staged, like he was trying to manipulate public opinion."

Mom nods, as if she's contemplating my words. "It's tough to navigate these feelings. Just make sure you pray about the situation."

"I do, Mom. You know I always try to," I reply, taking a sip of my lukewarm coffee.

"I've been keeping you and Donny in my prayers," she adds, her eyes sparkling with a hint of mischief.

I nearly choke on my drink. "Donny and me? Come on, that's ridiculous!"

A knowing smile spreads across her face. "I think there's something between you two that you've been fighting for a long time. Are you about ready to take your gloves off?"

"I don't know," I admit, lightly kicking my feet back and forth against the island. "I have my career to think about."

"Your career is important, but it's not the most important thing in your life. Everybody can see how you feel about each other," she insists, leaning forward, her elbows resting on the kitchen island.

"Not everyone," I retort, my voice tinged with frustration.

"I think you've finally discovered that elusive zing you've been searching for. Am I right?" she probes, her eyes glinting with encouragement.

My spine goes straight and my feet become still. "How could you possibly know that?"

"Didn't you kiss him the other day?" she asks with a wink.

"Mom!" My face has to be as red as Mom's fingernail polish. "You're right," I concede. "But I'm still not going to date him right now."

Chapter 33

Never in a million years would I have imagined I'd be about to have this nerve-wracking conversation with Clara. The phone rings for the third time. I bite my bottom lip. One more ring and I swear I'm hanging up.

Clara's warm, smiling face appears on the screen. "Hey!"

I force a smile that feels more like a grimace, but inside, I'm groaning with dread. "You know how I told you about the kiss with Donny the other day?"

"How could I forget that?" she laughs, her eyes sparkling.

Taking a deep breath, I press on. "I think I like him a little more than I've been willing to admit. Even to myself."

"Just so you know, I always saw the potential, even if you couldn't," Clara replies, with an eye roll.

"Did you now?" I lean closer to the phone, trying to get a better feel of Clara's mood.

"I've also noticed how your face practically lights up when you talk about him," she says, a smirk playing on her lips.

I shake my head. "I have no interest in dating a younger man, though. Plus, my career is taking off, and that has to come first."

"Too bad," she counters. "You felt the zing with Donny. Admit it. You. Have. Zinged."

"What if I have? That means nothing." Liar, liar, pants on fire.

"Ugh! Quit being so stubborn," Clara says, rolling her eyes in exasperation. "You remember how I fought my feelings for Archer, right?"

"Yeah, I sure do. You're welcome, by the way, for me

setting you up with your dream man," I retort. Clara never would've known Archer if not for me setting them up.

We both laugh, the tension in my shoulders easing for a moment. "Ha! Well, you're welcome for my mama birthing your dream man. Oh, and for me having your battery cables disconnected the other day."

"I can't believe you!"

"Hey, you set me up with Archer even though I fought it. Now it's my turn to make sure you follow your heart like you did with me."

"You'd better be glad I love you."

"Oh, I am. You'd better be glad I love you, too."

The doorbell rings, echoing through the house just as my phone buzzes with a text from Shawna, her message lighting up the screen. "Hey! Leo and I are both out front!" I glance at the clock. It's nearly nine.

"I need to get to the door. Leo and Shawna are here."

"I wish I could be there to help you."

"Me too, but professional designers can't help."

"Stupid TV show rules," she huffs.

We share a laugh before I hang up and head for the door, eager to see Shawna and Leo.

After two weeks of working side by side on the design, Leo, Shawna, and I are up to our elbows in paint. Leo glances around the foyer with a huge grin. "Can you imagine the people who have been in here?"

"I can picture people in fancy suits and frilly dresses walking around," Shawna says.

"Same. My goal is to preserve the historic and aesthetic value while adding a modern touch. I want to pay homage to the people who built this place and who worked so hard back then to keep it going."

"That's great! Thanks for having me here. It's pretty cool to be on TV. I'm really looking forward to it."

"No, seriously, thank you for all your help with this," I say, truly meaning it.

Leo scratches her chin, the sunlight streaming through the hotel window catching the sheen of her long black hair as she pushes a stray strand behind her ear. "I have a confession to make," she says.

"What's that?" I ask.

"I let Clara and Ruby talk me into pulling the Jeep's battery cable so you would have to ride back from

Pocahontas with Donny," she reveals, an apologetic smile creeping across her lips.

"Seriously?"

"Yeah, sorry about that." She shrugs, a hint of sheepishness in her eyes. "Clara was insistent that you were into Donny but just needed a little nudge in his direction."

My cheeks flush with heat at the thought. "I'll admit, Donny is adorable, and I do like him."

Shawna narrows her eyes. "Admit it, you think Donny Sharp has it going on."

"I mean, yeah, he definitely has it going on."

As I ponder the implications of our conversation, the cameraman steps around the wall, a buoyant smile on his face. He gives me an enthusiastic thumbs-up as he continues his exit from the hotel, leaving a trail of excitement in his wake from Shawna and Leo.

I turn to Leo and Shawna, my heart racing, and a knot of anxiety tightening in my stomach. "I hope he didn't just air that on live television," I say, trying to mask my rising panic.

My heart sinks as I realize if he did, there's no escaping the fallout. No biggie, I hope.

Chapter 34

Lisa Flowers claps her hands together. "Jane, I'm so happy you made it to the finale. This show is the highest-rated design competition ever for this network."

"That's amazing."

"Since we aired the behind-the-scenes segment last night with you saying Donny Sharp has it going on, people everywhere are invested in your life. If you play your cards right, you could have your own show."

Clutching the collar of my vintage blue-jean button-up shirt, I stare at Lisa, my mouth open wide. "Surely I misunderstood what you just said."

"Nope, you heard me correctly," Lisa says, pride evident in her tone.

I bolt out of my chair and pace across the room close to a large plant. "No, y'all may *not* put my private conversation on air."

"Private? Yeah, I don't think so." Lisa cocks her head, her expression a mix of irritation and disbelief. She lets out a frustrated sigh. "Jane, you were still mic'd up and standing in a designated filming zone. Anything you say is free to air. It's all in the contract."

My mouth dries out, and I struggle to keep the irritation out of my voice. "I didn't think you would air something so personal."

"Remember, nothing is truly private when you are in a designated filming zone." She enunciates the last three words.

"Please don't air something so personal again without my permission."

"I'm willing to agree to this, but you need to be more careful about what you say from now on. Understand?" Lisa's tone is serious, her eyes locking onto mine as if searching for sincerity.

"I will for sure watch what I say. Why would you say I could have my own show?"

"Let's not jump the gun just yet," she replies, her demeanor softening slightly. "But we definitely need to discuss this more after filming wraps up. I have another meeting to get to, so I'll catch up with you later. Thanks for understanding."

As I walk toward the hotel, the weight of Lisa's words lingers in my mind. My phone dings in my pocket, pulling me out of my thoughts.

DONNY

I hear you think I have it going on

JANE

They set a trap

DONNY

Sure

JANE

No, they did

DONNY

I believe you used the word adorable

I was under pressure

Ha! Heading to practice

See you soon

Tomorrow

And just like that, I can't wait for tomorrow.

❤

The following morning, I lower myself onto the plush area rug I selected for the foyer, its vibrant design contrasting beautifully with the muted tones of the surrounding decor.

As I settle in, my arch nemesis, Jackson Welch, struts inside. His jet-black hair is cut short and styled perfectly, and he is wearing a pair of cream joggers and a light-blue polo shirt. "Morning, Jane."

I glance at my red parachute pants, tight-fitting white shirt, and white sneakers, and smile. Our styles couldn't be more different. "Hey, Jackson. What's up?"

"I just wanted to say I'm glad you're back in the competition. It wasn't fair to kick you out because of something out of your control." He scratches the back of his neck.

"I appreciate that."

"Besides, you're the only one who has the slightest chance of beating me." His gaze takes on a predatory glint. "What fun is winning if you don't have to work too hard for it?"

"I'm speechless."

He looks down his nose at the rug I'm still sitting on. "What an interesting rug. I never would've chosen it, but you're braver than I am. Obviously."

Theodore walks in for our scheduled session, interrupting the smart remark on the tip of my tongue. "Morning, Jane," he greets, his voice warm with the energy that only morning people have. "Jackson, how are you?"

Jackson greets Theodore before smiling toward the stairs on his way out.

"Morning, Theodore," I reply, flashing a cheeky smile toward the cameraman who stands poised in the background, ready to capture the moment for our audience.

Theodore glances at the rug, his eyes lighting up with genuine appreciation. "I love the way the sprinkles of blue pop out against the golds and browns in the carpet," he remarks as he drops to the rug beside me. He runs his hand over the intricate patterns, and I can't help but feel a swell of pride at his praise. "Great job on this."

My heart skips a beat. It feels monumental, and the rush of validation stirs a mix of excitement and disbelief inside me. But then my gaze drifts across the room, and I realize I've stained the polished wooden staircase with two different shades of stain. A knot of anxiety tightens in my stomach as I hope he doesn't notice the glaring inconsistency. That's what Jackson must've been smiling at. Ugh! Hopefully, Theodore doesn't see it.

It looks like I'll be spending my evening scrubbing away at my mistake, trying to restore the staircase to its former glory before the world sees it.

Chapter 35

What I wouldn't give to fix up this entire hotel! It has so much potential, it's unreal. I spin around the room, and a goofy smile spreads across my face. Leo and Shawna took a break, and honestly, I'm glad to have a few minutes alone in here.

A single red rose appears around the door. My stomach flips as a grin flits across my face. "Who goes there?"

"It is I, fair maiden," Donny says as he steps into the

foyer.

Now my heart has joined my stomach in a gymnastics tournament. "Hi," I say, my tone breathless even to my own ears.

"Hi," he says, handing me the rose.

The cameraman appears out of nowhere, and he gets the shot of Donny handing me the rose.

I ignore the camera in my face when I really want to stick my tongue out at Eddie, the cameraman. "How's it going?"

"Good. Man, Jane, this place looks great."

"Thanks. I appreciate that. Leo and Shawna have been invaluable in helping me get it to this point."

"I'm glad you got over your jealous spell of Leo. My cousin."

I hold my finger up as I remove my mic. "Let's go somewhere more private." Once outside, I stop by a single-lane car wash before turning to Donny. "How did the show go?"

"It went well. Nothing crazy happened." Donny grunts as he leans his back against the red brick carwash.

"That's good, I'm glad you're back." I wave at a tall man and a short woman who're walking a black poodle. They wave back as they continue down the sidewalk. "The mayor has been excited to hear your band practice."

"Is that the only reason you're glad I'm back?" Donny crosses his arms before nudging me with his shoulder.

"What other reason could there be?" I scrunch my lips up.

"Let me see. The reason is that you think I have it going on. You want to kiss me. You want to date me," he answers in a sing-song voice, a hint of humor touching his lips.

I push him into the wall with a smirk. "Okay, Sandra Bullock, you need to be good."

"Always." He runs his hands through his long bangs. "The guys are pumped for Saturday."

"I bet there will be tons of people here."

"I'm excited. We all are. So, how are things with Theodore going?"

"He's been gone the past couple of days, and I've been slammed getting the foyer done, but so far, so good."

"I bet you've been busy. At least busy talking about how you find me irresistible." He jiggles his brows, and

I can't stop the grin from lighting my face.

The grin turns devious. "Oh, Donny. Don't you remember Lisa Flowers telling me to do what it takes to engage the audience?"

He pauses, the white of his eyes visible. "Wait, what?"

As I take a step closer to Donny, I lean next to his ear, my tone pouty and low. "You need to ask yourself if I was serious in what I said or not."

Leaning back, I run my finger down his jaw before sashaying away, leaving Donny with his mouth hanging wide open.

Frogs chirp a lovely tune as I stare into the dark night over the river. I push the porch swing back and forth, back and forth, as I think of my dilemma with Donny.

My phone rings.

"Hello," I answer on speaker.

"Hi there, Jane Bennett, superstar designer," Chance Banks, a guy I dated for a couple of months, says on the other end of the line.

"Chance? What's going on?"

"I was hoping we could talk. I'm back in Arkansas for good."

"What brings you back to Arkansas?" We called things off when he moved to Arizona for a job promotion.

"I got transferred back. It was way too hot in Arizona for me. I was hoping we could reconnect."

Before I could answer, Chance let out a yelp. "Sorry, I'm gonna have to call you back. I'm getting pulled over."

I hang up and glance at the door, only to meet Donny's wary gaze.

Chapter 36

My first instinct is to back away and run to my room with my tail between my legs. But that's not how I'll win Jane's heart. Chance Banks is my brother-in-law's cousin. He's older than me, has a professional job, and dated Jane briefly last year.

I don't like him at all. Well, that's not true. He's a good guy. But I'd prefer him to find someone else to meet up with.

"Sorry, I wasn't trying to eavesdrop." I hold up the

bag of Oreos. "Thought you might want a cookie."

She motions for me to join her. I hand her the bag. "You're right about that."

She tears it open and crunches into a cookie. "Where's the milk?"

"I'll get some."

"We can go together."

Together. I like the sound of that. Way better than the sound of Chance Banks talking Jane into meeting up. But I won't stand in her way if Chance is who she wants to be with.

"That is, if you're sure you want cookies. And milk. I love chocolate chip cookies, but there aren't many I won't eat."

I grin to myself as a hitch overtakes my belly. One thing I love about Jane is that she can ramble on and still be attractive. Honestly, there's not much of anything she could do that would make her unattractive to me. I even love the way she still shops at thrift stores so she can keep her eighties style going strong. She's nothing if not consistent. My stomach jerks. Did I just admit that I love Jane? The world around me spins, and I see stars. Even though people are talking, I have no idea what anyone is saying. I am in love with Jane

Gorgeous Bennett. Like, *really* in love.

When did my crush grow? Has it always been love? Do I even know what love is? I slide my arms around Jane. She hugs me for a second before backing away. Unable to stop myself, I grasp her hands, pulling her into another hug. She tilts her head, and our eyes tangle.

"We should go before the milk gets warm."

"I'm right behind you."

Back on the porch, milk in hand, we settle onto the swing. Jane dips a cookie into the milk and smiles at me. She pulls it out and bites half off before sticking what's left back into the milk.

After eating the other half of the cookie, Jane dips another one. "I saw where the girl who was obsessed with you tagged you on TikTok with an apology."

The old wooden swing creaks beneath us, swaying gently with the breeze as she seems to avoid my gaze.

"Yeah, that was unexpected," I say, shifting in my seat. I'm not out here to talk about Genny Weatherston. "Hey, I hope you know I wasn't listening in on purpose."

"Donny, it's okay. This porch isn't exactly private, so I get it," Jane replies, glancing around at the sprawling backyard, the golden light of the setting sun filtering through the leaves of the trees nearby.

"Are you going to do it?" I ask, waiting for her answer on pins and needles.

"Do what?" Jane furrows her brow, swirling the milk around in her cup.

"Meet up with Chance?" I lean in, studying her reaction.

When she meets my gaze, I see a flicker of interest. But is it for Chance Banks or me?

She looks away, her gaze settling on something near the water. "I don't know. Why?"

Her phone rings. Chance Banks again. "You should take it."

"I'll be back in a minute," she says as she answers the phone.

Needing some advice from a married man, I dial Jesse's number. "Hey, Donny," Jesse answers on the first ring. "What's up?"

"Jane's ex-boyfriend called her and wants to reconnect."

"Ouch. What does she think about it?"

Rubbing my temples, I sigh. "I'm not sure."

"Well, buddy, I can tell you women want to know

where they stand. If you don't want her with her ex, you'd better tell her you care about her."

"You're right, man, but I just have a hard time, I guess, because of our history. I mean, Jane has been Clara's best friend since we were little bitty."

"Just be honest with her. That's the best advice I can give."

"Yeah, I remember when you and Summer first started dating, and you were scared to tell her you decided to go to the police academy."

He chuckles. "I was so scared she'd break up with me after she told me she had no desire to date a cop."

"It all worked out, though."

"That's right, and if Jane is the one, it'll all work out with you, too."

I hang the phone up more determined than ever to tell Jane how I feel and to be serious about it. Because right now she probably thinks I'm a big jokester.

When she returns, I lick my lips, waiting for her to tell me what she and Chance decided.

"I think you should meet up with Chance if that's what you want." I attempt to make my tone more serious, so she knows I can be mature and reasonable.

Not that Jane and Chance getting together could

ever be reasonable in any world I live in.

She swivels around so that her body faces mine. A grin covers her face as she runs her index finger from my wrist to the end of my pointer finger. "Really? That's surprising."

My heart slams into my ribcage so hard I may have to dial 911. How is Jane sitting here as if she didn't just rock my world with a simple touch? By the grace of the good Lord, I find my voice. "It's important you have no regrets."

"Regrets?" She dips another Oreo into milk, cutting her eyes my way.

I follow her lead by dipping my cookie into milk. "Yes, when we're a couple, I don't want you looking back wondering 'what if' about anyone."

Her eyes widen as she chews the last of her cookie. "When we're a couple, huh?"

"That's right. When. Not if."

"Feeling cocky much?"

"I sure am. Now that I heard you call me adorable, I can't help but feel anything else."

"I may never live that down."

"Ha. Someone took that clip and turned it into a meme. It's all over social media."

"No way!"

"Yep, and you are adorable, saying I'm adorable."

"What am I going to do with you?"

I move the bag of Oreos and our cups of milk to the table and grab Jane's hands in mine. "First, you're going to meet up with Chance to make sure you don't have any leftover feelings for him."

"Okay. That's what I'm doing with Chance. What about you?"

If this woman knew how her words make me want to run to the preacher's house, she'd stop making her voice so soft and sultry. "Once you tell Chance to hit the road, you'll come back to me and fall into my arms."

Giggles flow from Jane, and she covers her mouth. "Fall into your arms, huh?"

Chapter 37

Donny caps his eyes on my face. "Yep. In all seriousness, I want you to be happy, Jane. But not with Chance. Does that make me a bad person?"

"I wouldn't say bad..."

"Growing up, I thought you were the prettiest girl I'd ever seen. My crush lasted for almost ten years. But what I feel now is no crush. I think you feel something for me, too, but I want you to be sure. Sure about me. Sure about us." He pauses, drawing in a deep breath.

Leo and Shawna bustle through the door. Shawna scoops a cookie out of the bag before looking from me to Donny and back again. She grabs Leo's hand and drags her into the cabin, announcing, "Leo, we have to stay inside. I think Donny and Jane are having a serious conversation."

"Let's give them some privacy."

Shawna's voice carries through the screen door. "Can we sit in the living room, though? I want to hear what he says to her."

Leo gasps. "Shawna, we don't need to eavesdrop."

"But I've been waiting a long time to hear what Donny has to say to Jane."

"Why don't we let them have their private moment, and we can ask them what happened in the morning? Does that sound good?"

"I guess. But I want some more cookies," she says before running back outside, snatching the bag of Oreos.

Donny watches her go before taking my hand in his again. "I told Dad I have feelings for you, and he suggested I study Ephesians 5. Since our chat, I can't tell you how many times I've read and studied that chapter. And every single time I read the part about men loving their wives as their own bodies, I know loving you that way would be so easy."

"Me?" I only thought I knew what a zing was. What I'm feeling now is a zing times a billion.

"There's no one else but you, Jane."

"Wow," I say in a whisper, my eyes burning with unshed tears.

"If you think there's even the slightest chance you still have feelings for Chance, I need you to be honest with me," Donny says, his voice steady.

I shake my head gently, looking down at the floor. "Oh, Donny, I never truly loved Chance. I had strong feelings for him. But it was never love."

"Well, I want you to be one hundred percent sure. Your happiness means more to me than my own," he adds, his eyes searching mine for the truth. "But in my heart, I still can't shake the feeling you don't belong with Chance."

I gasp, surprised by the intensity of his words. The warmth radiating from him is a comfort, stirring a swirl of emotions deep inside me.

"I'll let you get some rest, but I want you to think about what I said." He leans in, pressing a gentle kiss to my hand, his lips lingering for a moment longer than necessary, before he stands. With one final, lingering look, he walks out the back door and into the yard, leaving me enveloped in a heavy silence.

When I finally cuddle into bed, I close my eyes, replaying the events of the week. Maybe I can have a career and a man. Other women do it, and I'm just as strong as they are. With a deep breath, I turn on my playlist, and the familiar melody of Donny's band fills the room. Soon, the gentle voice of a green-eyed man sings me to sleep.

Chapter 38

Downtown DeValls Bluff is alive with excitement as the festival kicks off its first night. The main street is closed to traffic, transformed into a vibrant scene of colorful lights and joyful sounds.

A towering Ferris wheel spins against the twilight sky, its bright lights twinkling like stars, while the cheerful music of the carousel fills the air. In front of it, there's a long line of nearly twenty people waiting, their faces glowing with excitement. Various booths line the street, offering everything from homemade crafts to tempting snacks, each one bustling with people from across the state.

The evening breeze carries the sweet, familiar scent of strawberries, reminding me of Jane's signature fragrance. I can't help but inhale deeply, savoring the delightful aroma in the air.

Clara and Jane have been sharing laughter and whispers for the past three hours, their giggles echoing like music above the lively chatter of the crowd. Now, they stroll in front of me, their arms linked in a playful display of friendship, as Leo and Shawna walk beside me.

We catch bits of Jane and Clara chatting. "I'm really happy Archer's back is finally getting better," Jane says with a smile.

Clara replies, "Totally! He wishes he could be here, but traveling is a bit much for him right now."

"I get that." Jane nods.

Clara glances back at me, her brow slightly furrowed. "Hey, have you heard from Mom or Dad today?"

"Nope, but Gramma texted me earlier. She said she's having the time of her life on their cruise. Today they saw whales breach in the icy waters."

Clara smiles, her expression softening. "I'm so glad they took her to Alaska for her birthday. It must be such a breathtaking experience."

"I know, right? I would love to go to Alaska one day," Shawna chimes in, her eyes sparkling with excitement. "Imagine hiking through those stunning national parks and seeing all the wildlife up close."

Gregory Hill, my bandmate, playfully nudges Shawna with his elbow, a cheeky grin spread across his face. "Same here. Maybe one day we can go together," he suggests, his tone light and teasing.

Shawna's eyes widen, her mouth falling open in astonishment, but she remains silent, clearly taken aback by his boldness.

Just then, Jane swivels her head around, a small, amused smile tugging at the corners of her lips as she absorbs the unfolding moment.

I grab Gregory by the arm and pull him away from the group, my voice dropping to a conspiratorial whisper. "What are you doing, man? Are you really trying to flirt with Jane's younger cousin?"

He shrugs nonchalantly, his smirk unwavering. "Um, I'm flirting with a beautiful woman who is the same age I am. Why? Is that a crime?" he retorts, the playful glint in his eyes suggesting he's reveling in the thrill of it all.

Shawna spins around, her long chestnut hair swirling around her shoulders like a silky curtain. "Are you calling me beautiful?" she asks, her eyes wide with curiosity.

"I am," he replies, his tone light. "Surely you've been called beautiful before."

"Mama says I am," she responds with a hint of pride, her cheeks flushing a soft pink.

I lower my tone, glancing at Gregory. "Look, Shawna has been sheltered, so don't mess with her head," I warn him, knowing how easily his charm could blur the lines for her.

He holds both hands up in mock surrender, a grin tugging at the corners of his lips. "Okay, I get it. I'll leave her alone." But then he leans in, lowering his voice. "But I think she's so pretty."

"Think it from a distance," I reply firmly, casting an apprehensive glance at Shawna.

Shawna narrows her eyes at me, a hint of defiance in her expression. "Donny, you better stop that. Gregory can call me beautiful if he wants to."

Jane rubs Clara's stomach. "I can't wait to meet my little nephew or niece."

Clara hugs Jane close. "Same." She turns and winks at me, and I grin. What Jane doesn't know is that one day, I plan to make her this kid's actual aunt.

"Shawna, how about we go grab some cotton candy?" Leo asks.

Shawna nods, and they head away from us. I narrow my eyes, but Jane shakes her head. Yes, I know Shawna is twenty-two years old and not a baby. I don't know why I feel so protective of her.

Gregory watches her go before turning to me. "You didn't have to embarrass her like that."

"I didn't mean to," I reply, raising my hands defensively, a wave of guilt washing over me.

"Another thing," he continues, crossing his arms over his chest, "the guys and I feel the same way about Japan. They'll tell you when they get here. We never really wanted to go. It was more of a Sebastian thing. He was all about that trip putting the band on the map."

"Thanks, man. And I'm sorry I got smart over Shawna."

The tension between us eases as the mayor steps

onto the stage and announces the headlining band. Within minutes, a country tune about the beach fills the air.

I long to tug Jane close, but at least we're here together, and Chance is nowhere to be seen.

Chapter 39

After another morning doing interviews to promote this afternoon's finale, I can't believe this is my life. We go live in less than two hours. I pinch myself.

I'm super excited about the finale, then why am I standing here, watching Donny Sharp's lips, thinking about how soft they are? How did I go from "I'll never date him" to "I don't want to be without him"? Especially since we've not even technically been on a date. I guess we've been on one if I count the dinner at White's.

Donny steps up to the microphone. "Testing." He meets my gaze and smiles.

I groan. His dimples are going to be the death of me.

"What are you doing out here eyeballing my brother instead of getting ready for the finale?" Clara asks, laughter in her voice.

I grab my chest, my heart beating like a racecar. "Girl, you scared me!"

"Is it because you got caught ogling my brother?"

I jerk my eyes in her direction. "You. Are. Evil."

She puts up air quotes. "I will never date someone younger than me. Never."

"Donny and I aren't technically dating or anything like that. We're just spending time together because of the situation with his hand and how I hit him, and really, it's your fault that he came to the cabin when I was already there."

By the time I take a breath, Clara is holding her side, she's laughing so hard. "After that ridiculous speech they were forced to listen to, your little niece or nephew just kicked me in the ribs."

"As if."

When Donny belts out the song Alone by Heart, I have to physically stop myself from fangirling. Now I understand why that girl took matters into her own hands with him. Could I? Should I? I mean, not stalk him, but should I just tell him how I feel?

"Are you thinking about how good Donny sounds and looks right now? Hey, I'm used to girls going all mushy around him. You may as well join in on it."

"Stop that mess," I say with a grin.

Clara looks me up and down. "You look cute, by the way. I love the way you crimped your hair."

"I got another perm like they used to in the eighties." I glance at my jeans, ballet flats, and cute blue top. "And I found this outfit at a second-hand shop in Little Rock earlier this week."

"Well, I like it. It's so eighties but looks modern at the same time. Are you wearing this to the final?"

"Yep."

"Perfect choice!"

I wrap my arms around Clara. "Thank you for being my best friend."

"I will always be your best friend."

"Even if I have to eat my words about dating a younger man?"

"Especially then."

Unable to resist the alluring pull of curiosity, I make my way to the sitting room, eager to uncover Jackson's handiwork. As soon as I enter, my eyes bounce all over the place.

The space embodies the Craftsman style, highlighted by an array of meticulously selected period tables and chairs, thoughtfully arranged to invite conversation. Above, a grand chandelier dangles gracefully from the polished tin ceiling, its intricate design casting a warm glow throughout the room. At the heart of it all, a monumental fireplace stands as the room's centerpiece, exuding warmth and a timeless charm that beckons people to gather and share stories.

"Do you approve?" Jackson asks.

"It's beautiful."

"My girlfriend suggested making the chandelier this big, and I'm glad I listened. It makes the area complete. Don't you think?"

I nod as I continue ogling. "I can't help but think of the famous actress who stayed here in the fifties."

He looks confused as he changes the subject. "I stopped by your little foyer earlier and saw that you took care of the staircase."

"I did."

"You did a good job."

"Thanks. I'd better get back," I say, already walking away.

The new stain on the dark wood of the winding staircase shines. The turn-of-the-century sofa and side table look like they were made for this area. I spin around, satisfied there's not much more I can do to make the foyer perfect.

Theodore pokes his head into the room, surveying the intricate patterns that adorn the walls. "Beautifully done, Jane," he praises, a genuine smile spreading across his face.

"Thank you," I say, my cheeks warming at the compliment.

"You can definitely tell both your parents have design in their blood. This space feels like a reflection of your history," he adds, gesturing to the carefully arranged furnishings and the tasteful artwork that hangs above.

"For sure."

Theodore shifts around. "Would it be okay if I hang around after the competition is over?"

"Yeah, I guess that'll be okay," I respond, though I'm sure my voice carries a hint of hesitation.

"Have I offended you?"

"No, you haven't. I'm just concerned..." I trail off, fidgeting with the hem of my shirt.

"About?" he prompts.

"I don't know if you really want to know me or if you're using this situation to further your career," I admit, my gaze shifting to the floor, avoiding his eyes.

"Ouch."

I take a step closer to Theodore. "I don't even know you, and you don't know me. How could you say you care about me?"

"Because you're my daughter," he says, his voice softening. "I would quit the show right now if that meant getting to know you better. That's how much you mean to me."

The sincerity in his gaze is palpable. The moment I step into his arms, he releases a breath, hugging me tight.

Chapter 40

We go live in fifteen minutes. Clara runs a curling iron through a piece of my hair as I watch her in the mirror. I glance around my dressing room. Various flowers fill vases spread about the room. A lot of people are happy for me and wish me the best. I'm thankful, but my gaze lands on the dozen red roses from Donny, and I can't help but smile.

Clara runs her fingers through the back of my hair. "I can't get over how cute you look with curls and crimps like this."

I try to speak, but all that comes out is a squeak.

Within seconds, Clara lowers herself into a crouching position in front of my chair. "Hey, don't be nervous. Not only did you make it to the top two in a design competition you never thought you'd get into, but you are also Jane Gorgeous Bennett, and you've got this. I promise you deserve to be here."

I grin. "Jane Gorgeous Bennett?"

Clara giggles. "That's what Donny has called you behind your back since he was around sixteen, I guess."

A crack of laughter springs from me, easing the tension in my shoulders and neck. "That's good to know, I think."

One of the crew members sticks her head inside the room. "It's time."

I shift my weight in the chair and nod. "Coming."

Walter, the host, spends forty-five minutes backtracking and showing the audience what has happened over the past couple of months in the design competition. Then the moment arrives when he calls Jackson and me onto the stage. The same stage Donny will be singing on later this evening.

Donny catches my eye and winks. Mom gives me a thumbs up, and Theodore simply smiles. Clara lets out a whoop. I give her a mean mug she ignores, but it at least makes me feel better.

The host smiles a superstar smile. "Both of you have done an outstanding job on your designs." Shots of both rooms flash across an enormous screen behind the stage. "This has been the most interesting show I've ever hosted, and, Jane, I have you to thank for that."

Laughter and applause erupt from the audience. My face heats, but I manage to smile.

"Without further ado, the winner of Small Town, Big Design, is... Jackson Welch!"

My body flushes hot and cold. Forcing my lips into a small smile as I clap may be one of the hardest things I've done since I've been in this competition. If I wasn't on national television, I'd punch the wall.

Both of Jackson's hands fly up, covering his mouth. "I can't believe it!" He turns to me. "Jane, I just knew you had this in the bag since your dad is Theodore Baldwin."

Swallowing the stupid tears that threaten to flow, I turn to Jackson. "When he stepped down from being a judge, all that changed. Also, you're an amazing designer."

A pink tinge covers Jackson's cheeks. "Oh, and your design is so stunning."

I don't know what else to say, so I just hug him. "Congratulations. You deserve this win."

As the cameras stop rolling a little later, my mind races with what's next. I want to be taken seriously as a designer. But how can I get there after all the drama on set with my family? I straighten my spine. No matter what, I *will* get there.

Later that evening, Clara and I walk arm in arm down Main Street, the festival going strong around us. Carnival music comes from all around, making me crave a funnel cake. As we stand in line at the food truck, someone touches my arm. I startle as I spin around.

Chance Banks pulls me in a bear hug. "Jane!"

"Chance?" My forehead wrinkles as a sudden headache hits me. "What are you doing here?"

"I told you I wanted to see you again, remember?" he says, giving me a lopsided grin.

I try to get Clara's attention by tapping her elbow. "Yeah, but I told you I have a lot going on right now."

My eyes dart to Clara, but she's engrossed in whatever order she's making.

He takes a step closer to me. "I want to be here for you."

Clara turns around, holding a hot dog and a bag of chips. The dumbfounded expression she wears must mirror mine. "I didn't know you were in town, Chance," she says as she steps away from the counter. "Jane, will you grab the funnel cakes?"

"Sure thing," I say as the vendor hands me a plate and a super-sized lemonade.

"Yeah, I got back a few days ago." With a sigh, Chance shakes his head at me. "It really sucks that you didn't win."

I can almost feel Clara's back bristle. "She may not have won the finale, but she sure is better off than before she started."

Chance gives a one-shoulder shrug before laying his hand on my arm as we make our way through the crowd. "I was hoping we could talk later."

Part of me wants to tell Chance to get lost, but maybe I'm too nice.

Before I have time to respond, Donny's smoky voice carries across the festival. "This one is for Jane."

I spin around, my heart pounding in my chest as the piano chords for REO Speedwagon's Can't Fight This Feeling begin. As soon as Donny sings, I hand Chance the funnel cakes and lemonade. He calls my name, but I elbow my way through the crowd until I stand before the stage.

Donny drills his gaze into mine as he sings one of my favorite songs.

Chance appears by my side, looking between Donny and me. "Looks like I have my work cut out for me, huh?"

Chapter 41

A couple of hours later, it's quiet at the cab-in. Leo got a job offer earlier today, so she left for home directly after the competition, leaving Theodore to take up residence in her room. I'm not sure how I feel about that, but I guess I need to deal with my feelings.

Donny was still playing on the stage when we left the festival, which has left me lonely. I could wake Clara, but pregnant women need their sleep. And my

Aunt Olivia is not a night person. What about Shawna? I glance at her sleeping form and tiptoe out of the room as soft snores echo on the wall.

An owl hoots in the distance as I slip out the back door, easing it closed behind me. A billion stars litter the sky as I take a seat close to the shore, its current calm and peaceful.

A pleasant, earthy fragrance fills my senses as I lean my head back against the plush cushion of my reclining chair. I close my eyes, savoring the moment. I steal a glance at my phone screen, illuminated in the dim light of the moon, and decide to power it off, cutting myself off from the chaotic buzz of notifications. My social media is blowing up with messages and comments, and all I crave right now is a moment of peace and relaxation. It's surreal to think I have almost a million followers, a milestone that once felt like a distant dream.

I could easily stay here with nothing to entertain me but the moon and stars for the entire night. My lips part in a satisfied grin as I reflect on everything that's unfolded over the past few months. First, I made it to the top two in the competition for "Small Town, Big Design," a journey that tested my creative boundaries like never before. Second, I've developed a genuine friendship with Leo, who has become my confidant and creative partner in crime. And finally, I can't forget the thrill of discovering my zing. I have found the one who sends electric currents through my veins.

As I sit up straight in the seat, I realize that while I've acknowledged my zing, I have yet to claim my man. The nagging question tugs at me: what's wrong with me? Why am I hesitating to make that leap?

Just as I'm lost in thought, someone clears their throat, pulling me back to reality. "I was just about to knock on the door when I saw your phone screen light up out here," Chance calls out as he steps over a pile of rocks.

I inwardly groan. Not long ago, the sight of Chance striding toward me in his khaki shorts and a striped white and purple polo would have made me happy. Now, though, the only person I long to see is Donny Sharp.

Almost as if I had conjured him from my thoughts, Donny materializes on the walkway, his black t-shirt molded to his athletic frame and dark-washed jeans hugging his legs like a second skin. He walks with effortless confidence, each step resonating with a certain magnetism. "Hey, man, what's going on?" he asks Chance, a casual grin lighting up his features as he approaches.

"I thought I'd swing by to talk to Jane before I head out," Chance replies, shifting his weight from one foot to the other, his expression awkward. "Was I right to assume this is the Jane you dedicated that song to tonight?"

"The one and only," Donny replies, stepping right up beside Chance, a playful spark in his voice.

Chance bounces on his heels, eyebrows raised. "So, you two are together? Man, you could've given me a heads-up before I drove all this way."

I bite back a smile, letting the assumption hang. No way I'm correcting him now. "I did tell you I have a lot going on."

Donny flashes a wide grin and pats Chance on the back. "Hey, at least the festival was worth the trip. And you got to hear some real music."

Chapter 42

Jane keeps making eyes at me over the breakfast table. I bite my bottom lip as I shovel in a bite of biscuits and sausage gravy. "Miss Abigail, this gravy is the bomb."

"Thank you, Donny." She points her fork at me. "And stop calling me Miss Abigail. From the way you and Jane are eyeing one another, I bet you'll have another name for me soon."

Jane's head whips around, and her brows furrow at

Abigail. "Mom!"

Clara braces her forearm on the table. "Don't act so shocked. Everyone at this table sees it." She glances around the table. "Am I wrong?"

After everyone agrees, I put my hand out to Jane, and she lays hers on mine. "So, Jane and I have decided to get married. Tomorrow."

Abigail pushes herself to standing, shock on her face. "What?"

A giggle bursts from Jane as she continues, "Yeah, I'm wearing jeans and a t-shirt. And Donny is wearing his black shorts and ripped-up shirt he wears on stage."

With a snort, Abigail lowers herself into the seat. "You almost had me going."

I glance at Theo, and he's scrolling through his phone, a smile on his face. "Well, too bad. I just booked the church."

Abigail slaps her forehead. "Silly me, I should've already done that." Her eyes wander to Theo and stay on him a few seconds longer than Jane must've liked.

Jane clears her throat. "Okay, it's time for you two to separate. I think you're both bad influences."

Out of the corner of my eye, I notice Theo's smile. He seems so happy to have found Jane. After watch-

ing her grow up without a dad, I love that he's genuinely interested in getting to know her. She needs
this.

Theo's phone buzzes. He stands and glances at Jane.
"This is the producer for my show." He taps the screen,
and his expression turns serious. "Theodore Baldwin."

A few minutes later, he returns. "I have some news
and a proposition for you, Abby. The network wants
to sign me for a second season set in Arkansas, given
how wildly popular this competition was. They want
me," he glances at Jane, "and you to do it together."

"How is that a proposition for me?" Abigail asks.

"I'd love it if you would agree to be a part of the
show."

Jane holds her hand up. "The mayor asked me to
stay here for a few months to help fix up the rest of
the hotel. They want to open it for business."

Theodore nods his head. "That's fantastic. What
would you think about doing part of our show here in
DeValls Bluff? If you agree, I'll get with the producer."

Jane meets my gaze, and I nod. "Okay, see if they
agree, and we'll go from there. Mom, are you in?"

"I have my business, which takes up a lot of my time.
I really need to think about it."

"You could hire a designer to keep the business going and only be on the show part-time." Theo's tone is near pleading.

"I'll definitely think about it, but I'm leaning toward saying yes."

"What about you, Shawna? Donny?" Jane turns to me, her face brightening as she speaks. "You both wanna hang out here a bit longer to help me fix up the hotel? Good help is hard to find, you know."

"I'd love to!" Shawna bounces in her seat.

Draping a casual arm across the back of Jane's chair, I grin. "I can work from anywhere since I travel for my shows."

Clara brushes her palms together. "I'll have Archer remove this cabin from the rental pool for the foreseeable future. It's big enough for everyone. Does that sound good?"

"You're the best sister ever."

"And the best friend."

Jane's smile lights up the room. My very own Mavis and I'm her Johnny. I never would've compared myself to a cartoon character, but here I am.

Chapter 43

A few nights later, I know there's cookies call-ing my name somewhere in this house. Sure enough, there's a platter of homemade chocolate chip cookies that Summer brought over last night. I slip three onto a saucer and grab the milk.

"Hey, Chuck Norris, do you have a skillet, or is it safe to enter the room?"

At the sound of Donny's voice, a tremor shoots up my spine. I set the milk on the counter, my eyes crinkling into a smile. "I think you're safe. Want a cookie?" I ask without looking at him.

"I sure do. You grab the platter, and I'll bring the milk and meet you on the back porch."

"Okay," I say as I pour the cookies off the saucer back onto the platter. Our eyes meet, and I pause. Donny's black t-shirt and loose shorts are damp, and water droplets cling to his neck.

My throat clenches with a hard swallow. "How long have you been back?"

"Long enough to shower," he says, scooping up two cups of milk.

Back in the familiar swing on the back porch, my stomach settles down, and I think I can look at him without blushing. Until I try it. Heat rushes from the pit of my stomach, only stopping long enough to shoot an electric current through my heart before ending at my head. I imagine what it would be like to run my fingers through Donny's wet hair. Thinking about it intensifies the electricity in my heart.

Donny brushes his hand across my cheek. "I'm proud of you."

I blink, tilting my head to the side. "That means a lot. Even though I didn't win the finale, I'm thankful for the show."

He leans his elbow across the back of the swing, resting his cheek on his fist. "I imagine. Without it, you might not have met your father."

The intensity in is green-eyed gaze tugs at my heart. "There is that. But there's also you."

The corners of his mouth quirk into a huge grin. "Me?"

I flash a huge smile at him, as this reminds me of our conversation from the other day when I asked the same question. "I love you, Donny Gorgeous Sharp. Maybe I always have. All I know is you are my one." I scoot across the swing and lace our hands together. "My zing. You are the Johnny to my Mavis, and I will no longer fight my feelings. I can't. I don't want to be without you ever again."

Tears glisten in Donny's eyes as he locks his gaze with mine. He takes a deep breath before speaking, his voice warm. "I promise to love you like there's no tomorrow. I'll be all in for you, lifting you up and cherishing your heart with everything I've got, right until my last breath. Together, we can build an amazing life, always keeping God at the center." He gives my hand a gentle squeeze. "Because once you say yes to me, I'm all about making you happy and putting your needs first."

His gaze lingers on my mouth for half a second before his lips entwine with mine. I hang on to the kiss, running my hands through his hair.

As we gradually pull apart, an uncontrollable, goofy grin spreads across my face. Donny mirrors my expression, his eyes sparkling with warmth.

"I still remember the first time you caught my attention," he says, his voice carrying a nostalgic lilt. "We were tangled up in a wrestling match on the living room floor. As we rolled and tumbled, something shifted, and I no longer wanted to win. Instead, an overwhelming urge to kiss you hit me. At first, I was freaked out, so I kept my distance after that day."

"Is that why you suddenly stopped wrestling with Clara and me?" I ask, recalling the sudden change in his behavior.

"Uh, yeah," he admits, scratching the back of his neck, a hint of sheepishness creeping into his tone. "I didn't know how to handle those feelings at first. But not long after, I decided you would be mine one day."

A smile creeps across my lips. "I like the sound of that."

Chapter 44

Three Months Later

I tap my fingers on the weathered wooden side of the small fishing boat, my impatience mounting as he takes his sweet time fiddling with the bait, carefully threading the squirming worm onto the hook.

The gentle water from the slow-moving current lapping against the hull is calming, a subtle reminder of the lazy morning. I tilt my head back, letting the warmth of the sun kiss my cheeks as the golden rays cut through the wispy clouds, painting the sky in hues of pink and orange.

Turns out, fishing is my favorite pastime. There's something magical about the tranquility of being out here on the water with Donny. It's been our own little piece of the world to share.

Donny and I have been fishing at least six times since I moved to DeValls Bluff. He's still living in Little Rock for now, but he comes down whenever he gets the chance.

"How's it been working with Theo and Abigail?" he asks, casting his line with practiced ease.

She rolls her eyes. "Fine, but only if they'd stop flirting all the time. It's like working in a romantic sitcom."

I lean over the side of the boat, my hand splashing into the cool water as I retrieve a soda can that's bobbing near the surface. "Do you think there's something going on between them?"

"Of course, I do," she replies with a half-smirk, letting out a soft laugh. "But if there is, they're definitely not saying anything about it. I'm just here for the entertainment."

"Wouldn't that be something else if your parents got together?"

"It sure would." I move to the other side of the boat to sit in the cool shade beneath the trees' canopy, my feet casually propped against the boat's edge.

Donny pulls a pink rod and reel out of a package, his eyes sparkling as if he'd just opened a box full of money. "I have something for you."

I sit up straighter, perusing the shiny gift. "It's beautiful!"

"You should practice casting it."

"But it's so pretty and new. Maybe I'll wait until next time since I already have a pole."

"No, try this one. Please. I'll bait it up for you."

I smack my lips but nod as Donny unpacks the pole. After he turns his back, adding the bait, I cast it when a gleam catches my eye from the end of the hook. "What kind of bait is that?"

"It's new. Maybe reel it in and make sure I got it on right."

The moment I reel it in, I let out a squeal the deepest fish in the river probably heard. At the end of the line is a diamond ring.

I put my hand over my mouth, sobbing. Donny falls to one knee, causing the boat to rock. "Jane Gorgeous Bennett, will you do me the great honor of becoming my wife? My mate? The one I will always love, cherish, and protect even if it costs my own life?" His voice catches on the last few words as tears line his eyes.

Goosebumps pebble my arms. "I would love to marry you, Donny."

He lets out a whoop as he pulls the shimmering ring from the fishing line, the early-morning sunlight dancing on its facets and casting beautiful, colorful reflections all around. "Do you like it?"

"I love it so much," I say, my voice and heart full of joy. "You'd better be glad it didn't fall into the river. I can't believe you put it on a fishing line!"

With a cheeky grin, Donny shrugs his shoulders. "Oh, Jane, don't you know I'll do whatever I can to keep life interesting?"

"I bet you will, rockstar future hubby." With a crook of my index finger, I beckon him to come closer. "Now get over here and give me some sugar."

Donny angles his body toward me, so close that our knees brush against each other, creating a shared warmth that pulses between us. He leans in, his breath warm and inviting, making my heart race as we draw closer. Our lips hover mere inches apart. "I'm happy to oblige, ma'am," he replies, a playful smirk dancing across his lips.

With a quick shift of my body, our lips meet in a rush of warmth and sweetness, igniting sparks. I lose myself in the moment, just like I imagine Mavis did with Johnny.

Chapter 45

My soon-to-be father-in-law, Anthony Sharp, steals a quick glance at Donny as he smoothly merges the Ford Expedition onto the highway toward University Medical Center. "Son, I have to say, this drive to Vegas has been more pleasant than I thought it would be," he remarks, a hint of surprise in his voice.

Beside him, Krystal, my soon-to-be mother-in-law, leans in closer, her fingers softly rubbing the back of Anthony's neck. "I've really enjoyed the drive too.

The scenery is beautiful, and I can't wait to meet our grandson."

"Me too!" Donny's Gramma chimes in from the third row, her voice filled with excitement, as she adjusts her glasses after looking up from her phone.

Donny, sitting next to me with a playful grin, rests his hand on my knee before leaning in between his parents, his face lighting up. "Y'all, this has been worth it. I'm getting to live out a dream I've had since I was a kid," he shares.

Krystal turns to him and asks, "What dream, sweetheart?"

With a mischievous smile, Donny replies, "I always wanted to snuggle with Jane in the backseat." He draws me closer, wrapping an arm around my shoulders, and my cheeks flush with warmth.

Trying to hide my red cheeks, I bury my face against his shoulder and laugh. "Did you really make up being afraid to fly just so you could ride in the back seat with me?"

He gently kisses the crown of my head, his warm breath sending a shiver down my spine as his gaze lingers on my lips. "Nope, but this is the first time I've been thankful for my fear," he murmurs, his voice low and raw.

I brush my fingers across his cheek, feeling the roughness of his stubble against my skin, and a surge of excited contentment washes over me. In that moment, my heart races, and I blurt out what's on my mind. "I can't wait to be your wife."

Bringing our mouths within the same breathing space, he lets out a deep sigh. The raw intensity in his gaze sends a thrill through me, making me squirm slightly in my seat. "I love you, and I'm ready to marry you as soon as possible," he declares.

"I feel the same way," I reply, a smile spreading across my face as excitement bubbles within me. "Let's pick a date while we're waiting for our nephew to make his grand entrance."

"It's a deal," he says, a grin lighting up his features.

A few minutes later, Anthony parks, and we all unload, buzzing with anticipation as we head toward the hospital.

Archer meets us at the door to their room. "I didn't have time to text or anything, but Little Luca couldn't wait for y'all to get here."

My heart plummets to the floor with excitement. I haven't felt this elated since the day Donny proposed. We all take turns stepping into the softly lit room to meet the newest member of the family, little Luca. When it's finally my turn, I grasp Clara's hand, my pulse racing as I gaze, wide-eyed, at the tiny baby nestled in a cozy bassinet. His head is crowned with black curls, and his delicate features take my breath away. "He is the most beautiful baby I've ever seen," I whisper, my voice barely above a whisper.

Even though exhaustion marks Clara's face, she radiates love and joy. Her tired eyes sparkle as she gazes at her son. "I love him so much I can't put it into words," she replies, her voice thick with emotion.

"You did so good, mama," I say, my voice trembling as I fight back tears of overwhelming happiness.

With the boys occupied with Luca, we finally have the perfect opportunity for a girls' shopping trip, a much-needed break after the past week. Our fist stop, an adorable little vintage market.

Clara hands me a pair of vintage-looking blue jeans, their faded blue fabric exuding a nostalgic charm. The pocket stitching is slightly worn, exactly how I like my jeans. "Look how cute those are!"

Gramma nods as Clara disappears down another aisle. "Krystal, I think you had a pair just like those."

Krystal giggles as she checks the jeans out. "It's possible, that's for sure."

"Jane!" Clara calls out, her voice bubbling with enthusiasm as she races down the narrow aisle. "You have to see what I found!" Without waiting for a reply, she turns on her heel and dashes back the way she came.

Intrigued, I quicken my pace to catch up. Clara comes to a halt in front of a dress, its delicate lace catching the light. "Look at this eighties style dress!" she exclaims, her hands gripping the garment as she lifts it off the rack.

I take a deep breath, my heart fluttering as my eyes land on the gown. It's stunning! With a high-collared neckline that adds a classy touch, it really stands out. After securing a dressing room, Krystal helps me slip on the gown. She kisses my cheek. "I am so happy you're marrying my son."

"Me, too." I get out between sniffles. The natural waistline fits almost perfectly, and the long bishop sleeves flow beautifully, their delicate ruffles and lace dancing around. The fabric is a dreamy ivory chiffon that catches the light just right, revealing subtle hints of peach blush that give it a magical feel. I'm captivated by every tiny detail of this stunning dress.

Tears pool in the corners of Clara's eyes when I step out of the dressing room. "Oh, Jane, you are stunning. We may not have planned to go wedding dress shopping yet, but here we are, and I love it. Do you?"

"I'm shocked at how perfect it is," I say, bouncing on my toes.

"Magnificent!" Gramma adds. "Donny will fall over when he sees you in this beauty."

After I pay for the gown, we leave the store, and I find myself planning a Vegas wedding.

Chapter 46

The kitchen remodel project at the hotel is progressing well, and I can't help but take a moment to soak it all in. I spin around the room, admiring the gleaming countertops, painted cabinets, and the new, state-of-the-art appliances that gleam under the bright overhead lights. As I mentally go over my checklist for the day, ensuring that every detail is perfect, I can't shake the admiration I feel for Theo, who has played a major role in the remodel. I never understood the saying like father, like daughter as much as I do now.

An enthusiastic squeal behind me, and I turn to find my former design assistant, Nelly Harrington, beaming with delight. "This kitchen looks fabulous! You've done such a great job," she exclaims, her eyes sparkling.

"Hey, you helped!" I respond, grinning back at her.

Nelly nods, her expression softening. "I'm just so thankful you brought me back after the boating incident. I never expected to break my arm," she says, chuckling at the memory.

"Hey, listen," I say, playfully grabbing her arm. "I really owe you one. If you hadn't taken that unexpected dive off the boat, Donny and I might never have become so close."

"Really?" she responds, her eyes lighting up with curiosity.

"Absolutely. With you out of the mix, I needed Donny's help with all those projects on the houseboat," I reply.

"Wow, that's great to hear. So, I guess I should celebrate my unintentional splash, then," she laughs, a cheery sound that could brighten anyone's day.

"We're happy to have you here," Theo adds, wiping at his tailored gray slacks. "But not that you broke your arm."

"Definitely," Mom says. "Especially now that you're up for a part in a movie!"

Nelly pushes a few locks of purple hair out of her face. "I may not get it. It's been a while since I've acted in anything more than a commercial."

Mom's tone shifts to one of encouragement. "You'll get it. If not, a better opportunity will come along. I watched some of your TV shows last night, and you're a great actress."

Nelly's cheeks redden. "That was a long time ago. I was a kid."

"Even more reason to think you'll get this part. If you were that good an actress back then, just think how much you've improved over the years," Mom says, causing Nelly's blush to deepen.

Theo glances at his watch. "The camera crew will be here soon. Y'all ready for showtime?"

Nervous tingles of excitement run through my body. I'm so ready for the day because tomorrow Donny will be here performing at the alumni reunion. The morning can't come soon enough.

Stepping into the old high school gym is like entering a cherished piece of history. I can't help but admire the glass cases that proudly display the incredible achievements of past athletes. I'd give anything to have the letterman jacket displayed.

The shine of the buffed floors and the beauty of the immaculate wooden bleachers and walls create a warm, welcoming atmosphere. The walls, adorned with their mascot, a fierce golden rooster outlined in deep purple, represent strength and determination. Although the school merged with the Hazen district years ago, this gym continues to thrive as a beloved gathering place, hosting reunions every two years for all alumni of DeValls Bluff schools and other various events.

A tingle races through my body as my future husband strides confidently up to the microphone. The moment he belts out "Don't Be Cruel" by Elvis, that initial tingle erupts into an electric surge, a jolt of energy so intense that even Nikola Tesla would have been in awe.

Summer rests her hand on my forearm. "Wow, Donny can sing."

"I can sing, too," Jesse says with a playful grin. "Just wait until we're alone, baby."

Summer giggles. "It's a deal."

My heart is happy. Very happy to be here, working on the Castleberry Hotel, sipping sweet tea with our friends, watching my rocking hot man sing in his band.

As I approach the buffet tables that stretch along the back wall, I'm captivated by the tantalizing aroma of sweet sauce. My eyes light up at the sight of Craig's Barbecue, fresh fish, crispy fries, and a delightful array of other dishes. I load up two plates before heading over to the table.

While the council president delivers a speech, I hand Donny his plate and plant a kiss on the top of his head. "This looks yummy," I say.

After I set my plate down, Donny stands and pulls me close. "Yes, it does, Jane Gorgeous soon to be Sharp."

I guess Donny will never stop calling me by the middle name he gave me when we were kids, and that makes life even more delicious.

Chapter 47

The flight to Vegas takes less than three hours. As the plane begins its descent, Jane's small, warm hand intertwines with mine, her fingers fitting perfectly between mine like they were made to be there. "I can't believe we're getting married in two days," she whispers.

I nod, my voice lost in a whirlwind of emotions. The weight of this moment is almost surreal. I'm on a plane. My heart pounds in my chest, a wild drumbeat

I can't tell whether it's fueled by the thrill of my future wife beside me or by the gnawing fear of flying.

"Thank you for facing your fear of flying and getting on this plane for our wedding," Jane says, her voice soft yet earnest as she leans in to plant a gentle kiss on my cheek. The warmth of her touch distracts me from the unsettling turbulence that rattles the aircraft.

I lean into her touch, finding comfort in the connection we share, though a part of me is still acutely aware of the hard ground steadily approaching with nothing but the endless blue sky and swirling white clouds between us. "I can't believe I'm on a plane. That's how much I love you," I confess, my heart racing not just from the altitude but from the realization that I am about to marry the love of my life.

Mom, seated directly behind us, leans forward, her arm draped comfortably across the back of our seat. "I can't either," she replies, a smile softly illuminating her face.

From the other aisle, Theodore chimes in, his voice filled with enthusiasm. "Whatever makes you both happy is good by Abigail and me."

"Same for us," Dad says.

"And me," Shawna adds, causing a few chuckles from our family.

"Your aunt Olivia and I are thrilled," Jane's uncle Ray says.

Gramma shakes her pointer finger at us, her eyes sharp even though she's in her seventies. "I always knew you two would get together." She moves her gaze to Jane. "Remember how Donny used to follow you around like a lost puppy?"

"Yeah, but he was just a kid, and I always thought he was too young for me," she says, her gaze drifting to the window, where the soft glow of evening light illuminates her features.

"They say age is just a number, and I happen to agree," Gramma interjects with a playful twinkle in her eye, her voice laced with mischief. "My boyfriend is barely sixty-five, and let me tell you, he has more energy than half the people I know."

Dad gasps, his eyes widening in mock horror. "Mom! You can't be serious!"

"What? I'm not dead yet, son," Gramma replies with a cheeky smile, unfazed by his reaction. "By the way, we met on that fabulous trip to Alaska you took me on. Krystal met him once, too. She thought he was quite charming, actually."

With a grunt of disbelief, Dad glances at Mom, his expression filled with surprise. "You didn't tell me about that. We go on these adventures, and you keep this a secret?"

"Us girls have to stick together," Gramma says, nudging Dad with her elbow. "Besides, it was innocent. We had some good laughs over coffee, and now we chat over the internet, that's all."

I shift in my seat and take a moment to look at our families. "I don't mean to change the subject, but Jane and I want you all to know how much we appreciate your support," I say, my heart swelling with gratitude.

"Yes, we do," Jane agrees, her voice soft as she squeezes my hand a little tighter. "And I think you did mean to change the subject."

After our laughter dies down, we settle into a comfortable conversation about their trip to Alaska and the upcoming wedding.

As we step off the plane, Clara and Archer greet us. "I have never been so excited in my life!" Clara says. "You're already my sister, but now you'll actually be my sister."

"I know!" Jane says, hugging Clara before kissing

baby Luca.

Mom scoops Luca out of Clara's arms. "Hi, Luca, it's your Nana. Do you remember me?"

Clara shakes her head. "Mom, you just saw him three weeks ago."

"I know, but I've missed him."

"I can't believe Donny got on a plane." Clara puts a hand on her hip. "I tried to get him to fly to London when we were younger."

Abigail chuckles. "We had no idea Donny was afraid to fly."

Archer claps me on the back. "Clara has loved planning your wedding. Congratulations, man. I'm happy for you."

"Thank you, brother."

After a satisfying dinner of pizza and breadsticks, the house is calm. Only Jane, Clara, Archer, and I remain in the softly lit living room, with plates of leftover crusts scattered on the coffee table.

I fix my gaze on Clara, a teasing expression on my face. "I've got a bone to pick with you."

"Whatever for?" she asks, a playful glint in her eye.

"You told me that I'd have any woman I made mom's lasagna for hooked in no time," I emphasize the last part.

"And?" Clara replies, a smirk tugging at the corners of her lips as she shares a glance with Jane.

"I made it for Jane, and guess what? She was not hooked." I cross my arms, trying to hold back a grin, but the laughter bubbling from Jane and Clara makes it nearly impossible. I turn to Archer, who is leaning casually against the wall, a knowing smile playing on his face.

"What are y'all laughing at?"

Jane plops onto my lap, wrapping her arms around my neck. Her eyes sparkle, and she leans in closer, her breath warm against my skin. "You are so wrong. I was absolutely hooked."

I raise an eyebrow, trying to maintain my composure. "You sure didn't act like it."

With a swift motion, she presses a quick kiss to the side of my mouth, her lips warm and soft. "Oh, I was. Between the lasagna and the way you treated Shawna, I was a goner before I even knew it."

My heart races as I realize we will be married in less than forty-eight hours, and for a moment, everything else fades away.

Chapter 48

Two days later, as I step into the room for our wedding reception, I'm instantly enveloped in a vibrant atmosphere that echoes the electric energy of the eighties. Disco balls, adorned with sparkling facets, glimmer overhead, casting reflections that dance across the beautifully draped walls in an array of pinks, blues, and yellows that shimmer like a retro dream. Everywhere I look, there are hints of that iconic decade, from neon streamers swaying gently in the air to cassette tape centerpieces artfully arranged on each table.

With a soft chuckle, I can't help but admire the creativity of my future wife and sister, who have clearly poured their hearts into this whimsical celebration. It's a nostalgic tribute that transports us back in time, with classic hits from Madonna to Prince playing softly in the background.

At the moment, I couldn't be more thankful we opted for a small ceremony with family only. I'd hate to pass out in front of a bunch of strangers.

When it's time to take my place by the preacher, my fingers shake as I attempt to straighten my tie. A nervous pang strikes my middle, and I feel the need to pass out. I take a few deep breaths through my nose and out my mouth.

Finally, the pianist begins the Wedding March as Shawna and my bandmate Gregory make their way down the aisle, followed by Clara and Archer. Both Clara and Shawna are wearing hot pink bridesmaid dresses, while the guys are in simple black tuxedos. My heart pounds in my chest so fiercely that it's a struggle to catch my breath as I wait for Jane.

Once Clara and Archer take their designated places,

all eyes turn to the entrance where Jane and Theodore emerge. Jane looks stunning, her blonde ringlets cascading like golden waterfalls down her back, framing her face beautifully. The lacy vintage dress hugs her figure, the intricate patterns catching the light as she moves.

As Jane glides toward me with an enchanting smile, I can't help but grin back, warmed by the sight. She stops in front of me, and Edward Long, the preacher, offers a warm smile that lights up his features.

With a voice that resonates with sincerity, he proclaims, "Today, we gather filled with love and joy to celebrate the cherished union of Donny Sharp and Jane Bennett. Marriage represents not only a deep, unwavering love but also a profound commitment, a promise to support one another through life's ups and downs. It is the remarkable journey of two individuals choosing to walk side by side, creating a shared path filled with hope, laughter, and endless discovery."

"Let us bow our heads in prayer. Heavenly Father, we thank You for Your love and blessings on this day. We ask for Your guidance and favor upon Donny and Jane as they start their life together. May their love remain strong and last forever. In Jesus' name, Amen."

"Marriage is a beautiful joining of two lives into one. It is a heartfelt promise to love and support each other through every moment, both joyful and challenging. Marriage calls for commitment, understanding, and sacrifice from both partners, creating a shared journey filled with happiness and fulfillment. Donny and Jane, please exchange your vows."

My heart may burst as I fight the urge to tell the preacher to move quicker so I can kiss Jane as my wife. Instead, I meet her misty-eyed gaze and say the speech I've been practicing for days now. "Jane, I stand before you today with a heart full of love and confidence in our future. For more than half of my life, I have loved you, and I know that this moment is just the beginning of something incredible. Your beauty and grace inspire me, and I am proud to vow before God and all our loved ones to love, honor, and cherish you every single day of our lives together. I am ready to face whatever life brings, whether it be joy or sorrow, abundance or struggle, sickness or health. I promise to be by your side, offering my unwavering support. Together, we will navigate every experience with strength and unity, today and always."

Glimmers of unshed tears dance in the corners of

Jane's eyes as she gazes at me, her love shining. With a steady voice, she declares, "I, Jane Bennett, pledge before God and everyone gathered here today, to love, honor, and cherish you, Donny Sharp, every single day of my life. You are my zing, my one and only love, the heartbeat that completes me. In moments of joy and laughter, as well as in times of sorrow and struggle, through the ups and downs of wealth or poverty, in health and in sickness, I promise to stand by your side unwaveringly. I will support you always, through the trials and triumphs, for all the days of our lives."

Brother Edward nods, a gentle smile illuminating his face. "The ring you hold is not just a piece of jewelry. This ring represents unending love, a circle without a beginning or end, and serves as a tangible reminder of the promises you are about to make to one another."

He pauses and meets my gaze. "Donny, take this ring, and as you place it carefully on Jane's finger, repeat after me: 'With this ring, I give you my love and commitment, binding our hearts together for all time.'"

I swallow the burn at the back of my throat as I slide the ring onto Jane's finger, every touch leaving a trail of tingles. "With this ring, I give you my love and commitment, binding our hearts together for all time."

"Jane, place the ring on Donny's finger and repeat after me: 'With this ring, I give you my love and commitment, binding our hearts together for all time.'"

Jane radiates joy as she glides the ring onto my finger, her eyes sparkling with emotion. Her voice is soft and tender, barely above a whisper. "With this ring, I give you my love and my unwavering commitment, binding our hearts together for all time." she says.

"By the authority of God, I now pronounce you husband and wife. May God bless and protect your marriage all the days of your lives. You may now kiss the bride."

The moment our lips meet, the unmistakable opening chords of "Nothing's Gonna Stop Us Now" by Starship burst from the speakers, filling the room with the infectious energy of classic eighties music. After the sweetest kiss of my life, I lean back to meet my beautiful wife's sparkling, doe-eyed gaze. Her face lights up with a radiant grin as she begins to sing along to the nostalgic tune, her voice harmonizing perfectly with the melody.

I wrap my arm around her slender waist, pulling her closer as I join in, our voices intertwining like two melodies forming a duet. Within seconds, the entire wedding party rises to their feet, caught up in the infectious spirit of celebration, singing along with us.

Jane leans in, pressing another tender kiss to my mouth, her laughter bubbling up between verses. I can't help but let out a joyful whoop, overwhelmed by the sheer happiness of this moment. With her quirky love of all things eighties, her ability to wield not only a hammer but also a skillet, I can confidently say that life with Jane will be anything but ordinary.

Epilogue

T he air is filled with laughter as our entire family and close friends gather under the expansive blue sky outside the rustic cabin we bought from Archer and Clara.

Shawna, with her effervescent energy, claps her hands when Donny lifts the brightly wrapped gift she brought.

I shake a finger at Shawna. "We said no gifts, Miss Thang."

"I couldn't pass this one up," she says, sticking her tongue out at me.

"What is it? It's heavy," Donny says as he pulls an iron skillet out of the packaging. Loud barks of laughter reverberate around the yard. Everyone already knows the story of me hitting Donny with the skillet.

"That one is definitely for you, Donny!" Gramma announces with a playful grin.

Shawna, trying to contain her laughter, adds with a mischievous glimmer in her eye, "That's in case Chuckie takes another swing at you with a skillet! Now you can defend yourself!" The joke lands perfectly, and the laughter erupts anew, filling the yard with warmth. I may never live down the skillet incident. But I wouldn't trade the jokes at my expense for anything since that skillet is what ultimately brought us together.

Luca, my handsome nephew, coos at me. I snuggle him close, savoring the scent of this precious baby. I catch Clara's gaze, and she smirks. Reading her mind, I shrug because she was right. The love of my life had been there all along. We were already sisters through friendship, but now we are both thrilled to be actual sisters.

I sigh when I catch Theo eyeballing Mom like she's a piece of fried chicken and he's been on a deserted island for ten years, eating only berries. I recently started calling him Theo instead of Theodore. Maybe one of these days I'll call him Dad, but that can come later.

Mom tucks a few strands of hair behind her ear before watching Theo under hooded lids. She's just as interested in him as he is in her. But right now, we're all happy to simply get to know one another. Working on our new show has given us the opportunity to spend a lot more time together, and honestly, it's been great.

I'll forever be grateful for signing up for Small Town, Big Design. Not only do I know my dad, but I have the most amazing, hottest, sweetest husband I could've ever dreamed of.

Oh, and that zing I keep talking about? It's absolutely not showing any signs of letting up.

Acknowledgments

Writing Can't Design Me Love has been such a pleasure, and I know I couldn't have done it without my amazing support team. Each word I typed took me back to a time of my carefree youth, and I loved every minute of it!

A huge shout-out to Debbie Cook, the incredible Prairie County Museum Director, and to my distant cousin Ray Castleberry, for sharing more of the rich history of the Castleberry Hotel with me. I always love visiting the town where I grew up!

Regina, you're a true gem! Your feedback and suggestions have completely transformed my writing for the better.

A special thank-you to my super-talented illustrator, Nicole Roush! Jane and Donny are perfect!

And to my editor, Stephanie, you have a knack for making my words shine brighter!

Last but definitely not least, a heartfelt thanks to the

amazing folks of DeValls Bluff. So many of you have shaped me into who I am today, and I truly appreciate it!

XOXO

Leah

About the Author

Leah Brewer has written ten novels, two children's books, and several short stories. She also shares Christian articles on her blog, with almost fifty under her belt. Leah lives in Arkansas with her husband and family. She can't really get going until she's had her morning coffee—let's be real, that's a must! A trip to the beach brings her nearly as much joy as hanging out with her family. Romance is a big part of all her books, and she feels that stories really helped her heal after being diagnosed with ovarian cancer in 2019. Thankfully, she's been cancer-free for six years now! Leah enjoys writing happy-ever-after tales, aiming to make readers smile, strengthen their relationship with God, and help them find their happy place.

Check her out online at facebook.com/writingleahbrewer or at www.theleahjournal.com.

www.ingramcontent.com/pod-product-compliance
Lightning Source LLC
Chambersburg PA
CBHW021125070726
47591CB00014B/1326